MEET TH

Fortune of th

Age: 31

Vital statistic d rich.

Claim to Fame: Vice president of Robinson Tech, voted Most Likely to Break Hearts.

Romantic prospects: Excellent. Or at least they were until little Rosie came into his life. A three-year-old is not exactly an aphrodisiac.

"I'll admit it—I'm not the nurturing type. I should have said no when Zach asked me to be Rosabelle's guardian if anything should happen to him. But what were the odds?

Now I've got this crazy cute toddler and no idea what to do with her. I'm lucky that Zach's old girlfriend, Dana, has offered to help. I wish I had half Dana's maternal instincts. To be honest, I wish I had Dana in my arms—no, in my bed. But even I have more scruples than that. Zach's barely cold in the ground, and Dana deserves more than I am able to give her. My fantasies of playing house with her need to remain exactly that..."

THE FORTUNES OF TEXAS:
The Secret Fortunes—
A new generation of heroes and heartbreakers!

Dear Reader,

You have no idea how happy I am to be part of another Fortunes of Texas series. It's exciting to receive the story lines ahead of time, to meet the characters and see how each book will unfold. That was especially the case this year in The Fortunes of Texas: The Secret Fortunes.

If you're following the series, *From Fortune to Family Man* is the fourth book. I love stories with children, so I was delighted to have the opportunity to create three-year-old Rosie. The precocious child's mother gave her up at birth, leaving her biological father to raise her. But when her dad is killed in an accident, Kieran Fortune steps up to be her guardian. The handsome vice president of Robinson Tech knows his strengths. He's good at computers, he's good at making money and he's good at making love. Unfortunately, he doesn't know a thing about parenting.

Fortunately, Dana Trevino, who once dated Rosie's late daddy, steps in. Dana adores Rosie and is happy to help. But before long, Rosie is referring to Dana as Mommy and Kieran as Daddy. If that wasn't bad enough, attraction heats up between the mismatched couple. And they soon realize that the sexy businessman, the quirky librarian and their pint-size matchmaker just might become the perfect family.

I hope you enjoy reading Kieran and Dana's story as much as I enjoyed writing it.

Wishing you romance!

Judy Duarte

PS: I love hearing from my readers. You can contact me on Facebook at Facebook.com/judyduartenovelist.

From Fortune to Family Man

Judy Duarte

◆ **HARLEQUIN**® SPECIAL EDITION®

Special thanks and acknowledgment
are given to Judy Duarte for her contribution to
the Fortunes of Texas: The Secret Fortunes continuity.

Recycling programs
for this product may
not exist in your area.

ISBN-13: 978-0-373-62339-6

From Fortune to Family Man

Copyright © 2017 by Harlequin Books S.A.

HARLEQUIN®
™ www.Harlequin.com

Printed in U.S.A.

Since 2002, *USA TODAY* bestselling author **Judy Duarte** has written over forty books for Harlequin Special Edition, earned two RITA® Award nominations, won two Maggie Awards and received a National Readers' Choice Award. When she's not cooped up in her writing cave, she enjoys traveling with her husband and spending quality time with her grandchildren. You can learn more about Judy and her books at her website, judyduarte.com, or at Facebook.com/judyduartenovelist.

Books by Judy Duarte

Harlequin Special Edition

Rocking Chair Rodeo

Roping In the Cowgirl

The Fortunes of Texas: All Fortune's Children

Wed by Fortune

Brighton Valley Cowboys

The Cowboy's Double Trouble
Having the Cowboy's Baby
The Boss, the Bride & the Baby

Return to Brighton Valley

The Soldier's Holiday Homecoming
The Bachelor's Brighton Valley Bride
The Daddy Secret

The Fortunes of Texas: Cowboy Country

A Royal Fortune

The Fortunes of Texas: Welcome to Horseback Hollow

A House Full of Fortunes!

Visit the Author Profile page
at Harlequin.com for more titles.

To Michelle Major, Stella Bagwell,
Karen Rose Smith, Marie Ferrarella,
Nancy Robards Thompson and Allison Leigh.
I can't think of a better team of authors
to work with on a continuity series.

Chapter One

As Kieran Fortune Robinson stood with the other mourners at the Oakdale Cemetery, the Texas sky was a stunning shade of blue, the sun was bright and a cluster of birds sang from their perch in the nearby magnolia tree. But the spring day was dismal, the mood somber.

Three weeks ago, Zach Lawson had been thrown from a horse and suffered a skull fracture. As soon as Kieran had gotten word of the tragic accident, he'd rushed to the hospital to visit his best friend and to offer his support to Zach's parents.

"Only family is allowed to visit patients in the ICU," a nurse had said.

Zach's father had slipped an arm around Kieran

and clutched him with a firm grip. "This is my second son."

In a way, that claim had been true. Sam and Sandra Lawson had treated Kieran as a family member ever since Zach had brought him home to visit during their first winter break at college. A born and bred city boy, Kieran had actually enjoyed the time he'd spent at the Leaning L, even though his busy schedule hadn't allowed for as many visits as he might have liked.

Oddly enough, he and Zach hadn't had much in common, other than a quick wit, a love of sports and a competitive spirit. They'd met on the football field their first semester at Texas A&M and had become fast friends. Other than that, they were as different as a cowboy and a techie could be.

Zach had been an only child, while Kieran had seven brothers and sisters, although that number seemed to be constantly growing, thanks to his dad's years of philandering and the illegitimate half siblings who'd increased their ranks.

And there lay their biggest difference of all—the men who'd fathered them. Sam Lawson was a rancher of modest means who owned a small spread outside Austin. On the other hand, Gerald Robinson, a quirky tech mogul who'd once been known as Jerome Fortune, had built a computer company into a billion-dollar corporation.

After graduation, Kieran had become a computer analyst and eventually the vice president of Robinson Tech. On the outside, it might appear that he'd done his family proud, and in a sense he probably had. But to this day, he felt a lot closer to Zach's parents than he did his own. And that was why Sam's announcement to the hospital staff that Kieran was his second son had touched his heart in a warm and unexpected way.

But nothing had prepared him for what he saw when he approached Zach's bedside, where his once vibrant buddy lay unconscious and hooked up to a beeping ventilator.

If there'd been a chance that Zach might pull through, that he'd be able to go home to Rosabelle, his three-year-old daughter, they all would have found their hospital vigil easier to handle. Still, Sam and Sandra clung to each other and held on to their faith, praying for a miracle that never came.

Zach had remained on life support for two long weeks before his parents finally accepted the fact that their only child, a son born to them late in life, was virtually dead. And now here they were, at the cemetery, saying their final goodbyes.

Kieran stood beside Zach's parents, trying to be the second son Sam had claimed he was and to offer his support. But he wasn't sure how much help he could be. Sandra and Sam, both in their seventies and not in the best of health, were overcome by grief.

What really tugged at Kieran's heart, though, was three-year-old Rosabelle, who held her grandma's hand, her little brow creased as if she was trying to understand all that was happening around her. But how could she, when even Kieran found it so unsettling, so unfair?

A monarch butterfly fluttered by, weaving through the mourners as if trying to lift the spirits of those who'd come to pay their last respects.

After the pastor of the community church finished the eulogy, little Rosie pulled her hand away from her grandma's and reached for Kieran, silently requesting that he pick her up.

He did so, holding her close, wishing what little comfort he had to give would help.

"My daddy went to heaven," Rosie whispered.

"I know, honey." Kieran rested his head against hers, catching the light fragrance of her baby shampoo.

"I'm gonna miss him," Rosie added.

"Me, too." Zach's death was a huge loss that would affect them all.

"Look!" Rosie pointed to the orange-and-black butterfly that now landed on a spray of yellow roses. "It's a flutterby."

"I see it," he whispered, not bothering to correct her pronunciation. What did it matter anyway? He was just glad that she had something to hold her interest, to keep her from thinking about her loss, about not ever seeing her daddy again.

Kieran glanced through the crowd and spotted Dana Trevino, the woman Zach had been dating at the time of the accident. Her long, red hair was swept up into a tidy topknot, reminding him of a librarian. In that plain black dress, she looked like one, too.

A grad student and a research librarian at the Austin History Center, Dana wasn't anything like the women Kieran dated. Not that she wasn't attractive. She had a pretty face and a warm smile. At five-foot-five, she also had a willowy build, although she tended to hide it behind loose-fitting skirts and conservative blouses.

Still, Kieran had thought the cowboy and the librarian an odd match, although he suspected that Dana had been drawn to Zach's country charm and his Will Rogers style, which had given him a combination of wisdom, common sense and humor.

To be honest, Kieran wasn't sure what it was about Dana that had appealed to Zach. They'd never talked about it, but there must have been something special about her.

Still, for some reason he'd never thought their relationship would last. But who was he to judge? He never dated anyone longer than a couple of months, so he had no idea how to even define words like *special* or *long-term*.

As the stoic rep from the mortuary thanked everyone for coming, Sandra Lawson turned to Kieran. "Will you come back to the house with us? Sam and I want to talk to you." Her eyes filled with tears, and her bottom lip wobbled.

"Of course," Kieran said, although he suddenly felt compelled to pass little Rosie to the couple, hurry to his Mercedes and get the hell out of Dodge. But like Sam had told the hospital staff, Kieran was their second son.

Thankfully, he seemed to have already shed most of his tears in the hospital. By the time Zach's organs had been donated to give others a chance at a new and better life, Kieran's grief had seemed to subside.

He stole a peek at Dana, who appeared as prim and proper as ever. She clutched a wadded up tissue in her hands, but no tears filled her eyes.

Had she, like Kieran, done most of her crying in the weeks and days before the funeral? Had she also begun to let go of Zach and move on?

"This concludes the service," the mortuary guy said. "The family would like to invite you all back to their house for refreshments."

Kieran wasn't the least bit hungry, but he could sure use a drink—a stiff one.

Sam slipped his arm around his wife. "You about ready to go, honey?"

Sandra merely nodded, then blotted her eyes with a lace handkerchief.

"Can I ride with Uncle Kieran?" Rosie asked.

"Your car seat is already in our car," Sandra said. "It'll be easier if you ride with us."

Sam placed a hand on Kieran's shoulder. "You're coming home with us, aren't you, son?"

"Yes, of course. I'll meet you there." Kieran brushed a kiss on the little girl's cheek then passed her to her grandparents.

As Sam, Sandra and Rosie walked away from the graveside, Kieran remained a little longer so he could say a final goodbye to his best friend.

The monarch butterfly was still fluttering about. When it landed on top of the spray of red and white carnations covering the casket, he glanced to his right, where Dana continued to stand.

"Are you going to the Lawsons' house?" he asked.

"Yes, I promised them I'd be there."

It wasn't a surprise that Sandra and Sam wanted—or needed—to hang on to everyone and everything that reminded them of Zach.

"How've you been?" Kieran asked. "Are you holding up okay?"

Dana turned and caught his eye, a slight smile chasing the grief from her face. "I'm doing all right. After the last two weeks…well, that was tough."

To say the least.

"I feel so bad for Rosie," she added.

"So do I."

"At least she and Zach had been living with Sam and Sandra. That should help her adjust to not having her daddy anymore."

Kieran sure hoped Dana was right. Again he studied the redhead, noting a simple, wholesome beauty he'd missed seeing before. She'd implied that she was adjusting to her own loss, but he wondered if that was really true or the kind of thing people said when they struggled for the right words.

"Sandra mentioned that you'd been at the ranch with them earlier today," he said.

"I went to help some of the ladies from her Bible study prepare food for after the service."

"Do you need a ride back?"

"No, I have my car." She nodded toward a white Honda Civic parked about ten feet from his black

Mercedes. It wasn't a fancy car or the latest model, but it was clean and recently polished, the wheel rims shiny.

Funny what things a guy noticed at times like these.

"Then I'll see you back at the house," Kieran said.

Dana smiled—not a smile that was joyful and happy, but one that was filled with compassion.

Was *that* what Zach had seen in her?

Actually, standing there with her now, the afternoon sun casting a glow on those auburn strands of hair, Kieran noted that she had a natural beauty that was almost alluring. But he shook off the inappropriate assessment as quickly as it awakened. Dana had been Zach's girlfriend, and even though he was gone now, Kieran wasn't about to overstep the bounds of male brotherhood.

As he got into his car, he made up his mind to do whatever he could to help the Lawsons move on with their lives.

Growing up in the Robinson family, Kieran had learned that money could fix just about anything. But all the gold in Fort Knox wasn't going to make things better or easier for him. Not when so many different feelings were in play and he'd always made it a point to avoid any touchy-feely stuff.

Still, while he might fall miserably short in his attempt to offer Zach's family his emotional support, he'd do his best.

He owed his best friend that much.

* * *

Dana had managed to hold back her tears during the funeral. But once she climbed into her car, her eyes welled.

She reached into the pocket of her skirt, pulled out the wadded tissue she'd stashed there earlier and blotted her tears.

Would she make it through the day without breaking down? She certainly hoped so. She wanted to stay strong for Sam and Sandra.

How are you holding up? Kieran had asked just minutes before. It seemed to be a regular question she'd been faced with…at school, at work and, most recently, at the Leaning L while she'd helped the church women prepare the food for today.

She really didn't blame people for assuming she'd been devastated by Zach's loss. She mourned him, of course, but she wasn't the grieving fiancée they thought her to be. They'd dated six months, but in fact, she wasn't sure she'd even been his girlfriend. She'd certainly found him attractive, and she'd adored his sense of humor. But it was his family life that had appealed to her the most. That was the reason she'd continued to date Zach after she realized he wasn't Mr. Right. She suspected Zach had known it, too.

His parents had created a warm, loving home on the Leaning L, and they'd always made her feel welcome. In addition, she adored Rosie, Zach's sweet, precocious daughter. Since her mother had signed over full custody to Zach right after birth, that pretty much made Rosie an orphan, just like Dana was.

When Dana was twelve, she'd lost her parents in an accident. Without anyone who was either willing or able to step up and take her in, she'd gone into foster care.

Fortunately, Rosie wouldn't have to worry about that. The Lawsons had always been a big part of her life, so it wasn't like she'd be completely uprooted and shipped off to another home to live with people she didn't know. Dana took great comfort in that.

When she arrived at the Leaning L, she parked next to Kieran's Mercedes. It was only natural that he'd be invited back to the Lawsons' house. He and Zach had been the best of friends, even though the two men had been so dissimilar—and not just when it came to the clothes they wore, the music they liked or the social circles in which they ran.

Still, they'd been very close.

Much closer than Dana and Zach had ever been.

Before Dana could climb the wooden porch steps and let herself in, Kieran swung open the front door as if he'd been waiting just for her. Then again, she'd been right behind him.

"Come on in." He stepped aside so she could enter the small, cozy house that had always reminded her of the kind of place a ranching family might have lived in during the 1950s, with its rough-hewn paneling, the overstuffed, floral furniture with crocheted doilies over the armrests and a rag rug on the floor. It was all very Norman Rockwell. The only thing missing was a big, boxy television with a small black-and-white screen.

Maybe that was another reason she liked this

house—well, the vintage feel as well as the warm welcome she'd always received.

As she crossed the threshold, she caught a whiff of Kieran's cologne, something musky and woodsy, reminding her of a lazy summer day in the mountains. Something undoubtedly expensive and sold at only the finest stores in Austin.

"Sandra took Rosie to her room for a nap," Kieran said. "The poor kid could hardly hold her eyes open."

Dana acknowledged the comment with a nod, then scanned the living room, where the pastor of the church and several close family friends had gathered. They were seated on the sofa as well as on some of the chairs that had been moved from around the linen-covered table in the adjoining dining room.

The women from Sandra's Bible study and Dana had arrived early this morning and prepared the food, which would be set out as a buffet. Before leaving for the service, they'd stacked blue paper plates, white napkins and plasticware at one edge of the rectangular table, and placed a bouquet of spring flowers in the center.

Sam greeted Dana with a hug. "I'm glad you're here. Sandra and I wanted to talk to you as well as to Kieran. As soon as Rosie is sound asleep, we can go into the kitchen, where it'll be more private."

"Of course." Dana had no idea what they intended to say, but she was glad to be included in what seemed like a family discussion. She shot a glance at Kieran. Their gazes locked, their sympathies clearly united.

Moments later, Sandra entered the living room,

her eyes dry, yet still red-rimmed. "Rosie's finally taking a nap."

Sam nodded, then lifted his right hand, directing them to the doorway that led to the kitchen. "Shall we?"

When they entered the small, cozy kitchen, the counters lined with cakes and platters of cookies, memories slammed into Dana, causing her to pause in the middle of the room. One mental snapshot after another struck, the first one reminding her of the cold, rainy night last winter when she'd joined Sam, Sandra and Zach to play cards. The memories of times spent in this very room clicked in her mind as if she were watching the scenes on an old nickelodeon— the morning she'd helped Sandra bake cakes for the church bazaar, the afternoon she'd washed a bushel of apples that had come from trees in the family orchard, then learned how to make and can applesauce.

This particular kitchen, with its light green walls, white Formica countertops and floral printed café curtains, was also where Dana had last seen Zach alive and well. Sandra had invited her to dinner just three days before the accident. They'd had pot roast, carrots, mashed potatoes and gravy...

Dana shook off the memories before she fell apart and cried for all she'd lost. She'd loved her visits to the Leaning L, but now that Zach was gone, she might never be invited back.

Sandra, always the hostess, asked, "Would anyone like coffee?"

"Let me serve it for you," Dana said.

Normally, Zach's mom would have declined the help, but this wasn't a normal day. She took a seat at the antique oak table, practically collapsing in her chair.

Dana placed cream and sugar on the table, then filled several mugs with hot coffee and passed them out to Sam, Sandra, Zach and the pastor of the Oakdale Community Church, who'd been asked to join them in the kitchen. Since Dana preferred tea, she passed on having anything at all to drink.

"Last night," Sam began, "we… That is, me and… my wife…" His voice wobbled and cracked. He cleared his throat, paused a beat, then looked to the minister.

Pastor Mark nodded, then pushed his mug aside. "Sam and Sandra read over Zach's will last night, and they have a concern as well as a heartfelt request."

Dana still had no clue where this conversation was heading, but it was obviously in a direction the older couple needed their minister's help expressing.

Pastor Mark Wilder, who'd served his congregation for the last thirty years, scooted back his chair and got to his feet as if he was preparing for a sermon. "Sam and Sandra believe that Zach's wishes should be followed, but they also know he hadn't expected to die so suddenly or so young. And their biggest concern is for little Rosabelle."

Dana had no doubt about that. The couple adored their precious granddaughter.

"As you know," the pastor continued, "Rosie and Zach have been living with Sam and Sandra for her entire life. So the Leaning L is the only home she's ever known."

Where was he going with this? Dana assumed Rosie would stay with her grandparents. After all, she'd just lost her father. Who else would take her? Where else would she live?

Oh, no. Surely her mother hadn't resurfaced. From what Zach had told Dana, her pregnancy had been unexpected and unwanted. She'd planned to give her baby up for adoption, but Zach had refused to sign the paperwork, insisting that he wanted sole custody of their child. The woman had agreed and then walked away without a backward glance the moment she'd been discharged from the hospital.

Dana stole a glance at Kieran. The expression of concern he'd been wearing moments earlier had morphed into one that almost appeared panicked.

It wasn't until Pastor Mark completed his speech that Dana realized why.

"Zach gave custody of his daughter to Kieran."

Chapter Two

Kieran hadn't been sure the Lawsons had even known about the existence of Zach's will, but he had. He'd also been well aware of Zach's wishes when it came to who would raise Rosabelle. He just hadn't planned to bring it up, especially now.

When Zach had first mentioned his visit to the attorney and had asked Kieran to be Rosie's guardian if the unthinkable should happen, Kieran had laughed. Sure, he'd been honored to be chosen, but he'd known there had to be someone much better qualified than him to finish raising Zach's daughter.

What did Kieran know about kids—or parenting?

He didn't have any insecurity about his competence to do anything else. As one of the legitimate offspring of Gerald Robinson, aka Jerome Fortune

Robinson, he was certainly capable of taking care of her financially. He was a millionaire many times over and a damn good computer analyst. He was also good at making and investing money. But he was a man who knew his strengths, and parenting was not one of them. Hell, he certainly hadn't had the perfect example of either a mother or father while he grew up. And he'd told Zach as much.

But Zach had disagreed. "If something ever happens to me," he'd said, "there's no one else I'd trust to take care of my daughter."

Kieran would have mentioned Rosie's biological mother, but the flighty brunette was completely out of the picture. She'd gladly signed over full custody of the newborn to Zach and had never looked back.

"It's just a formality," Zach had said. "We'll both be dancing at Rosie's wedding."

At the time, Kieran had believed that was probably true, so he'd reluctantly agreed. But obviously neither of them had foreseen the accident that would change everything.

Kieran, who actually liked having Rosie refer to him as her uncle and had no problem assuming that easy role, blew out a ragged sigh as he looked at the people around the room. "I knew about Zach's will, but neither of us expected him to die so soon."

"Sandra and Sam are hoping that you will hold off on exercising your right to custody," Pastor Mark said. "At least while Rosie is so young, and the loss of her father is so recent."

Kieran hadn't planned to assume custody, although the Lawsons probably didn't know that. And he wanted to put their minds at ease as well as his own. "If Zach could somehow talk to us right now, he'd agree that Rosie would be better off living with the two of you. Your bond with her is the strongest, now that he's gone. We can discuss the legalities later. But in the meantime, if there's anything she needs, anything at all, just say the word. I'll make sure she gets it."

Sandra's eyes overflowed with tears. "I'm so glad you feel that way, Kieran. We love that little girl with all our hearts, and she's..." The grieving mother and grandmother sniffled. "She's all we have left."

It might sound as if he'd made a huge concession, yet even though he adored the sweet little girl, he was actually relieved that she was going to continue living with Sam and Sandra on the Leaning L.

"We'd also like both of you to remain a part of her life," Sam added, looking first at Kieran, then at Dana. "Especially over the next few months, while her loss is so fresh."

"Of course," Dana said. "I'd hoped you'd allow me to continue visiting her—and you, too."

"Honey," Sandra said, gazing at her son's girlfriend, "over the past six months you've become the daughter I never had. I've enjoyed having you around, even if it wasn't as often as I'd have liked." Then she looked at Kieran. "I hope you'll come by regularly, too. I know your job keeps you busy, but..." A tear slipped down her cheek, and she paused to wipe it away.

But she didn't need to finish her words. Kieran

knew what she meant. He'd make it a point to come around more often than he had in the past. "I'll never be too busy for Rosie or the two of you."

"See?" The pastor placed a hand on Sam's shoulder. "I told you all we had to do was pray about it, and everything would work out."

Kieran wasn't very religious, but he appreciated them putting in a good word with the man upstairs. As far as he was concerned, this was working out for the best—for everyone involved.

"Why don't you go back into the living room?" he suggested to the grieving couple. "I'll help Dana get the food set out."

"That's so sweet of you," Sandra said as she got to her feet. "I feel funny not being the hostess, but..."

Dana slipped her arms around Zach's mom. "I know you do, Sandy, but let me take over your duties today. Besides, I have help." When she glanced at Kieran, he nodded his agreement.

"Come on," the minister said. "It's time for people to show you their love for a change, just as you've done for them in the past."

After the Lawsons and Pastor Mark returned to the living room, leaving Kieran and Dana alone, Dana said, "I hadn't realized Zach gave you custody."

"I'm not entirely sure why he did."

"He considered you his best friend."

Kieran had felt the same way about Zach, but still, what had he been thinking when he'd asked Kieran to step up and parent Rosie? He was a diehard bachelor and not the least bit family-oriented.

Sure, he loved and respected his siblings. But seriously? He would make a lousy parent.

"Just so you know," Dana said, "I agree that it's in Rosie's best interests to stay on the ranch with Sam and Sandra, but you need to consider something."

Kieran never made rash decisions. What did she think he'd failed to think about?

"Sam has heart trouble, and Sandra's health isn't very good. I'm not sure how long either of them will have the stamina to keep up with an active three-year-old."

She had a point, and while he had no idea what the future held, he was glad the couple wanted Rosie—and that they would be able to raise her, at least for the time being.

As Dana moved about the kitchen, pulling salads from the refrigerator and serving spoons from the drawer, Kieran watched her work. He was drawn to her hair, especially since the color reminded him of autumn. She usually wore those long red locks pulled into a topknot or woven into a twist held up with a clip. He'd seen her with it hanging down once, and it nearly reached the small of her back.

He'd always thought of redheads as being a little feisty, but Dana was more serious and a little old-fashioned. She was also bright and the studious type. At least, he'd always had that assumption because she was a graduate student and a researcher at the history center, so it was an easy jump to make. Either way, she wasn't the type of woman Kieran dated.

When Dana turned away from the kitchen counter with a bowl of macaroni salad in her hand, she caught Kieran studying her. For a moment, something stirred between them—a spark of some kind. Maybe a flash of chemistry. He'd dated enough to know when an attraction was mutual.

But if he was right about what he'd sensed, she seemed to get over it a lot faster than he did.

"Is something wrong?" she asked.

"No." *Hell, no.* He'd merely zoned out, caught up in a momentary fixation. He shook off his wild thought. "I… I just wasn't sure what to do next."

"Would you take this salad, along with the others on the counter, to the dining room and place them on the table?"

"Sure." Glad to have a job to do, one that would take him out of the kitchen and away from her, he took the bowl and did as instructed.

What was the matter with him? Even if he did find Dana attractive and interesting, she'd dated Zach. It wouldn't be right to think of her in a…well, in a romantic way.

So he'd better get his mind on either someone or something else. Quickly.

Dana reached into the drawer nearest the oven and pulled out a couple of pot holders. But she couldn't help glancing over her shoulder to see Kieran carry the first of the salads out to the dining room. The man might be well-dressed and gorgeous, but he was completely out of place in a kitchen, let alone one that was built in the 1950s.

Even when he wasn't dressed in a stylish gray Armani suit, the corporate vice president seemed to be cut from a different bolt of cloth than Zach. Kieran was made from expensive silk, like the fancy yellow tie he was wearing, while Zach had been made out of rugged and durable denim.

It was impossible not to compare the two men, to note their good qualities or admire their close friendship, although now that Zach was gone, there was no longer any reason to.

Dana returned to her work and pulled a ham from the oven, leaving two casseroles still baking inside.

When footsteps sounded in the open doorway, the kind made by Italian loafers and not cowboy boots, she turned to see Kieran return, his hands now empty.

"What next?" he asked.

She put the hot pan on the stove top, then set the pot holders on the counter. "Would you mind slicing this ham?"

"No, not at all."

"There's a serving platter in the small cupboard over the fridge. There might also be a couple of trivets in there. I'll need them to hold the casserole dishes."

His brow knit together. "What's a trivet?"

She couldn't help but smile. He'd probably been raised with a housekeeper, a cook and a nanny, so it was no wonder that he didn't know his way around a kitchen. But she had to give him credit for trying to help and to fit in. "A trivet is a small little rack that keeps a hot dish from resting directly on the table."

"Got it." He brushed past her, leaving a soft trail of that mountain fresh scent in his wake.

She couldn't help taking a second whiff, appreciating his unique fragrance. But that's the only arousing awareness she'd allow herself. She shook off her momentary attraction, took the pot holders in hand again, removed the two casseroles from the oven and placed them on the stovetop.

After Kieran set the platter on the counter, he removed the trivets from the cupboard. "Why don't I put these on the table so they'll be ready for those hot dishes?"

She thanked him. Then, in spite of her resolve to keep her mind off him and on her work, she watched him go. She'd never been interested in men like Kieran, although she had to admit he was more than attractive. At six feet tall, with light brown hair and blue eyes, he was a killer combination of bright and sexy. Most women wouldn't think twice about setting their sights on him, but Dana was more the down-home type. And she knew most men considered her to be a little too quirky to notice her in a romantic way.

In addition to the obvious, Kieran was also a member of the renowned Fortune family. And Dana had no family at all.

Of course, that didn't mean she'd been left destitute. Before their fatal accident, her parents had set up a trust fund for her, and last year, on her twenty-fifth birthday, the money had been released. She'd used most of it to purchase and to renovate a run-down house in Hyde Park that was built in the 1940s.

Still, even though she was a property owner and had a small nest egg, she wouldn't fit into the social circles in which Kieran and his family ran—nor would she even want to try. Not when her idea of a perfect afternoon was a trip to an antiques shop, where she scoured vintage photos, or a lazy walk through flea markets, where she searched for hidden treasures.

No, she'd feel completely uncomfortable hobnobbing with Kieran and his rich family and friends. Heck, she sometimes felt out of place in 2017 Austin, which was one reason she loved walking in her quaint, historical neighborhood.

So why complicate matters when she liked her life just the way it was?

"I'm finished," Kieran said, as he reentered the kitchen yet again.

Dana was finished, too. Not just getting the food ready, but comparing the different lives she and Kieran lived. Besides, even if she ever did consider going out with a man like him, it would never work out. From what she'd heard, Kieran dated a lot of gorgeous women, and Dana would never agree to be one of many.

She had a good life—and a busy one. She wasn't lacking anything other than a family of her own. And now that the Lawsons had invited her to come around more often, she'd be able to maintain and nurture the relationship she had with them.

It might not be the perfect setup for the holidays and other lonely days, but it was close enough to be a darn good substitute.

The call Kieran had been dreading came only a week after Zach's funeral, while he was in his office at Robinson Tech.

"Sam's in the hospital with angina," Sandra said. "It's pretty serious this time, and I'm not sure how long he'll need to stay. They're talking about surgery."

"Is there anything I can do?" Kieran asked.

"I have a babysitter at the house with Rosie. The granddaughter of a neighbor. The girl is good with kids and responsible, but she's only fourteen. She'll be able to handle things for a while, but I have no idea how long I'll need to be here with Sam."

"Don't worry about Rosie," Kieran told her, even though his own concern about the child's well-being, especially with him in charge of her, was mounting by the second. "I'll pick her up and relieve the sitter. But if you don't mind, since I'm not too far from the hospital, I'll stop by to see you and check on Sam first."

"Thanks, Kieran. He'd love to see you. He's on the third floor, in room 312."

"I'll be there in twenty minutes—maybe less."

Sandra paused a beat then asked, "What would we do without you, Kieran?"

He could ask her a similar question. *How in the world will Rosie be able to get by without* you?

"I'm happy to help out whenever and however I can," he responded.

"Bless you, honey. I'll see you soon."

After disconnecting the line, Kieran told his assistant to cancel an afternoon appointment and to reschedule tomorrow's board meeting. Then he left his high-rise office and drove to the hospital. The direct route he took reminded him of the times in weeks past that he'd traveled that same stretch of road on his way to see Zach in the ICU, hoping and praying that his friend would have made some improvement during the night, only to find that he hadn't.

Kieran felt that same cold and heavy weight of dread and fear now.

Sam has heart trouble, Dana had said last week, *and Sandra's health isn't very good. I'm not sure how long either of them will have the stamina to keep up with an active three-year-old.*

He'd known Dana was right, but he'd hoped the older couple would be able to keep Rosie for another few years—maybe even until she graduated from high school.

Was it already time for him to step in and take full custody of Rosie, as unready as he might be?

Maybe Zach's parents only needed him to provide temporary help and babysitting duties. Once Sam was feeling better and returned home, Sandra would want Rosie back again. Then Kieran's life would go back to normal. He convinced himself that was the case.

It would only be for a few days. He could handle child care duties for that long.

"I got this," he said out loud, hoping the sound of his voice would provide all the assurance he needed.

Yet those words, interlaced with the doubt that plagued him, were still ringing in his ears when he entered the hospital lobby. As he started toward the elevator, he spotted Dana coming out of the gift shop holding a yellow ceramic vase filled with brightly colored flowers.

She wore a simple black skirt and a white sleeveless blouse. Once again, her hair was pulled up in a topknot, with two turquoise chopsticks—or were they knitting needles?—poking out of it.

When she saw him, she broke into a smile that dimpled her cheeks. Again, he was struck by her simple beauty, something he'd failed to notice when she'd been with Zach.

"I take it Sandra called you," he said.

"Yes, she did."

"I guess this is what you meant when you told me you were concerned about Sam's health."

Dana blew out a soft sigh. "Yes, but I was hopeful that the doctors had his heart issues controlled by medication."

Kieran had hoped that was the case, too.

"I just stopped by for a quick visit," he said. "I told Sandra I'd relieve the babysitter and keep Rosie for a few days. Once Sam is released and ready to go home, I can take her back to the ranch."

"You may need to keep her longer than that. The doctor mentioned surgery, and those 'few days' could end up being more long-term."

"Yes, I know." Kieran was trying to prepare himself for that possibility. He glanced down at his leather loafers, then back into Dana's eyes. There was no need to lie or to pretend that he was ready to be a parent. "To tell you the truth, I'm a little nervous about being Rosie's guardian. As much as I adore her, I've never spent much time with kids."

"I can understand that, but you'll do fine. Zach wouldn't have chosen you to step up if he'd had any concern about that." Dana's eyes, a stunning shade of blue, filled with something akin to sympathy. "Not that I'm an expert on child rearing," she added.

"That's just it," Kieran said. "I'm great at giving piggyback rides and playing hide-and-seek for an hour or two. But being her legal guardian means choosing just the right preschool and knowing when she needs to see a pediatrician." Damn. Just the thought of doctor visits brought on a whole new worry that filled his gut with dread. "What do I do if she gets a fever or a tummy ache?"

And then there was the whole idea of shots, immunizations and making her take liquid medicine that tasted nasty.

Worry and fear must have altered his expression because Dana said, "You'll do just fine."

"Thanks for the vote of confidence."

She placed a soft and gentle hand on his shoulder, which sent a rush of warmth to his gut, chasing a bit of his fear away. "And remember, it's just a few days at this point. There's no need to borrow trouble."

"That's easy for you to say." He offered her a half-hearted grin, although he really did appreciate her support.

"If it'll make you feel better," she said, "I'd be happy to stop by your place so I can visit Rosie and give you a break at the same time."

Kieran would take all the help he could get, even if it was just an occasional visit. "I'd appreciate that, Dana. Before you leave I'll give my business card, along with my address."

The hand that had been resting on his shoulder slid down to his back, giving it a rub that suggested she wanted to provide him with comfort and understanding. But her touch, the trail of her fingers, triggered a spark of heat he hadn't expected. Nor did he have any idea what, if anything, to do about it.

"You'll do fine," she said.

God, he sure hoped she was right. But he couldn't very well remain in the hospital lobby, talking to a woman who'd sent his thoughts scampering in an entirely wrong direction. So he nodded toward the elevator. "Are you ready to visit Sam?"

"Yes, let's go." Dana fell into step beside him, but they didn't speak again until they reached the third floor.

As the doors opened up, Kieran said, "Here we are."

They started down the corridor together, their shoes clicking and tapping on the tile floor. Still, they didn't speak.

When they neared room 312, they spotted Sandra walking out the door and into the hall.

"How's Sam doing?" Kieran asked her.

"About the same. The doctor has ruled out by-pass surgery for the time being, and he's responding to treatment. But Sam has a few other health issues they'd like to get stabilized before they dishcharge him. So it looks like he'll be here for a while."

"What about you?" Kieran asked. "How are you holding up through all of this?"

Sandra took a deep breath, then slowly let it out. "I'm a little tired, but I'm doing all right. My blood pressure is higher than usual, which is a little concerning. My doctor would like me to get some rest and stop worrying about Sam. But that's not easy to do."

Under the circumstances, Kieran didn't suppose it would be. Not when Sandra had their granddaughter to worry about, too.

"I'll plan on having Rosie indefinitely," Kieran said. "Once Sam is feeling better, just say the word and I'll bring her home."

Sandra's eyes filled with tears. What she couldn't blink away, she dried with her index fingers. "As much as I hate to let Rosie go, especially when I fear it could end up being permanent, I really have my hands full with Sam right now."

"I'll take good care of her," Kieran said. "And if it makes you feel better, Dana promised to help me." He gave the attractive redhead a nudge.

Dana slipped her arm around Sandra and drew her close. "That's right, Sandy. I know how difficult this must be for you, but don't worry about anything or anyone except Sam—and yourself."

"We'll just be a phone call or a short drive away," Kieran added.

"Thank you." The older woman again swiped at her teary eyes. "That's probably for the best."

Kieran knew they'd made the right decision all the way around, although he still wasn't sure about his capabilities as a guardian, let alone as a paternal role model. But he'd do his best by Rosie.

"Don't worry about a thing," he told Sandra, although his gut twisted at the thought of being on his own with Rosie.

But, hey. He'd just take it one day at a time.

"Sandy," Dana said, "is there something I can do to help you? Do you want me to bring anything to you from the house? Or, if you give me a list, I can run errands or stop by the market and pick up groceries or whatever."

"Since I don't have to worry about being home with Rosie," Sandra said, "I'd like to camp out here at the hospital for a while. So, yes. If you don't mind, there are some things you can pick up from the house and a prescription that's ready at the pharmacy."

While the women continued to work out a game plan of sorts, Kieran looked up at the ceiling as if he could see through it and beyond, as if he could somehow connect with Zach and ask for his forgiveness. *I'm sorry I lied to your mom. I have no idea how to provide for Rosie's needs.*

But he made Zach—and himself—a promise right

then and there. He would do his best to provide everything Rosie needed—come hell or high water and damn the cost.

Chapter Three

Dana hadn't planned to visit Kieran and Rosie until the weekend, but less than twenty-four hours after running into him at the hospital, she changed her mind.

He'd admitted to being nervous and uneasy about his ability to fill Zach's shoes. In spite of the assurance he'd given Sandy, Dana suspected that he wasn't feeling nearly as comfortable taking care of a three-year-old as he might want everyone to believe.

So after putting in a full day at the history center, she drove across town to the high-rise building in which Kieran lived. She and Zach had once attended a party here, where they'd hobnobbed with socialites, techies and corporate types.

They'd moved about the well-dressed group, holding their drinks in hand and making small talk. Zach might have appeared to be a simple cowboy, but his wit, humor and charm had carried him through the evening, and he'd fit right in. Not so with Dana.

Sure, everyone had been kind and gracious to her, even when the only things she could think to say had to do with a new exhibit at the history center. She'd smiled and nodded, as if all was right in her world, but she'd felt lost, like a street urchin on the snowy lanes of eighteenth-century London.

Okay, so it really wasn't that bad. But she'd felt out of place among the rich and successful crowd.

And now, after parking across the street in the public lot next to a busy Starbucks, she began to have second thoughts about her surprise visit.

What had she been thinking? She shouldn't just drop in uninvited. Maybe she should head to the pop- ular coffee spot instead. She could purchase a venti green tea and call it a day.

Then again, Kieran had said to come "anytime." She sat in her parked car, pondering her options.

What if he wasn't home?

Maybe she should give him a call. She reached into her purse, pulled out the business card he'd given her yesterday and read the personal contact information he'd written on the backside. Then she dialed his cell.

He answered on the third ring, although his voice sounded a little…tired. Or was he stressed?

"Are you up for a visitor?" she asked.

"If the visitor is *you*—and if you're talking about coming over *now*—I wouldn't mind a bit."

"Actually, I'm standing outside your building."

"Then come on up. I'm on the tenth floor, number 1014. My condo is on the east side, just to the left of the elevator doors."

"All right. I'll see you in a few minutes." She grabbed her purse and locked the car. Rather than jaywalk, she strode to the corner, waited for the green light and crossed the street to the impressive, curved building of glass and steel.

The doorman, a dapper, uniformed gentleman in his mid to late fifties, stood at the entrance. He must have been expecting her because he knew her name and greeted her with a smile. "Good afternoon, Ms. Trevino. Mr. Fortune said to send you right up."

She thanked him, then headed to the elevators. Once inside, a flutter started in her stomach and continued to build on the ride up to Kieran's luxury condominium, reaching a peak by the time she rang the bell.

The door swung open almost immediately, but when she caught a look at the handsome man, who appeared more than a little haggard, her momentary nervousness dissipated.

His mussed hair suggested that he'd just woken up from a long winter's nap, although she suspected he'd been raking his fingers through it more often than usual. He wore a black T-shirt and a pair of gray gym shorts, but she doubted he'd been working out. At least, not in the usual way. And even though his current appearance wasn't the least bit stylish, nor was he as impeccably put together as she was used to seeing him, it didn't make him any less attractive.

"I'm glad you're here." He stepped aside for her to enter. "Come on in."

She might have complied, but it looked as if an entire toy store had exploded in his living room. In fact, there was so much clutter on the floor she could hardly take a step for fear of tripping over something.

"What's all this?" she asked.

"Stuff I bought for Rosie."

Dana surveyed the results of his shopping spree—a blue-and-white doll house, a tiny pink kitchen setup along with plastic food items and a little red shopping cart. Puzzle pieces, crayons, books and a variety of stuffed animals littered the room.

Five different dolls of various hair color, skin tone and sizes were lined up on his dark leather sofa, each with a pink teacup in her lap.

"Where's Rosie?" Dana asked. "Or is she somehow lost in this mess?"

"She's been running on full throttle all day and finally went to sleep five minutes ago. But I have to tell you, I probably need a nap more than she does."

Dana furrowed her brow. It was after five o'clock. "Why'd you put her down for a nap this late in the day?"

"I didn't plan it that way. Every time I asked if she was sleepy, she told me no. Finally, she crashed on her own. I found her curled up on the floor in the guest room, next to her new toy box. I was afraid she'd wake up, so I covered her with a blanket and left her there."

Dana had no idea what to say. Kieran had admitted that he didn't know anything about kids, and she'd had no reason to doubt him. But she'd never expected anything like this, and she couldn't help but laugh at the absurdity.

"What's so funny?" he asked.

"Nothing." At least, not anything she wanted to actually say out loud. Poor Kieran looked as though he was ready to drop in his tracks, too. "Apparently, you've had a busy day."

He rolled his eyes. "You have *no* idea."

Dana continued to scan the room, just now noticing a pink motorized kiddie car parked in the dining area. Seriously? Kieran had purchased a big, outdoor plaything like that when he didn't even have a yard?

"This is mind-boggling," she said. "What'd you do? Take Rosie shopping and let her have free rein with your credit card?"

"No, I picked this out myself, along with some new clothes for her and a toddler bed. That's all in the guest room, which is where she'll sleep while she's here."

Apparently, Kieran had accepted the fact that Rosie's stay might not be temporary after all. "Did you purchase all of this today?"

"No, I bought it yesterday, before I picked her up from the sitter. I asked Karen, my assistant, to suggest a place I could find everything she might need, like toys, clothes and furniture. And Karen suggested Kids' World, which is supposed to be a popular place for parents to shop. I was able to get it all taken care of in less than an hour. The delivery guys brought it this morning."

"Talk about one-stop shopping."

"Yeah, that was the idea. I didn't have much time to get everything Rosie is going to need."

Children needed more than just toys and games. The most important thing was love, and that wasn't something Kieran could purchase.

Dana again scanned the clutter, unable to even guess how much all of this had cost him. For a woman who'd spent years in foster care, she couldn't fathom the extravagance.

"This must have cost you a year's salary," she said. Well, maybe not *his* salary, but certainly that of a grad student and research librarian.

"I'll admit, it wasn't cheap. But that doesn't matter. I just want Rosie to be happy while she's here."

Dana hated to criticize him for trying to do what he thought was best, but he needed to know that he'd wasted both his time and his money. "I hate to disappoint you, but Rosie probably would be just as happy with a picnic at the park, complete with peanut butter and jelly sandwiches. Or even a trip to the library for the preschool story hour, especially if she could also check out a few books and maybe a Disney DVD to bring home."

"For what it's worth," he said, "I did get a few of these things on sale. And they also delivered the whole kit and caboodle for free."

"And you think that means you got a bargain?"

Dana laughed again. "I'm surprised the happy owner didn't volunteer to carry it here on his back."

"Okay, so maybe I overdid it a little."

"You think?" Dana covered her mouth with her hand, hoping to stifle another laugh.

Kieran blew out a ragged sigh. "Okay, I probably blew it. But my heart was in the right place."

She had to agree with that. The man was not only wealthy and successful, but apparently generous, too.

"Don't just stand there," Kieran said. "Come on in." He moved aside the pink plastic shopping cart as well as the child-size kitchen, making a pathway for her. "Can I get you something to drink? I have every kind of fruit juice imaginable as well as Gatorade, punch and soda pop. Oh, there's also chocolate milk. But if you're up for something a little stronger, like I happen to be, you have your choice of beer and wine. I also have a full bar in the dining room."

"Actually, wine sounds good to me."

"You got it. What's your preference? Red or white?"

"Whatever's easiest."

"I have a sauvignon blanc in the fridge."

"Perfect."

"Have a seat." He directed her to the marble counter in the kitchen with a set of sleek black barstools. And she complied.

While Kieran uncorked the bottle, Dana scanned the interior of his home. She tried, in spite of the dolls and toys that littered the living room, to remember what his bachelor pad had looked like when she and Zach had attended his party.

The modern furnishings were both expensive and impressive. The artwork that adorned the walls and the sculptures that were displayed throughout also must have cost plenty, which made her suspect he'd hired a decorator.

What a contrast it was to her quaint little home, which she'd decorated herself, mostly with items she'd purchased at estate sales and antiques stores.

"There you go," Kieran said, as he placed a glass of chilled wine in front of her.

"Thank you." She took a long, appreciative sip and watched him move about the kitchen, with its state-of-the-art stainless-steel appliances that would please a master chef, and prepare a plate of crackers, cheese and grapes.

Did he usually fix dinner for a woman while they both enjoyed a glass of wine? Did he play soft, romantic music in the background?

Not that it mattered. But she had to admit she was curious about the women Kieran might bring home, the ones he found attractive. Did he prefer tall, leggy blondes? Maybe shapely and voluptuous brunettes?

Or how about quirky redheads?

She chased away that wacky thought as quickly as it crossed her mind. A man like Kieran Fortune wouldn't be the least bit interested in a woman like her. And while she found him more than a little appealing, he really wasn't her type, either. Still, she was intrigued by the handsome, dedicated bachelor who, according to Zach, claimed that he'd never settle down.

Yet here he was, apparently becoming a family man. How was that going to work out for him?

He removed a longneck bottle of Corona from the fridge, opened it and took a drink before sitting in the barstool next to hers.

"So tell me about you," he said, his gaze warm, his expression suggesting genuine interest.

She could understand that. Even though she'd dated his best friend for the past six months, Zach's priority in life was his daughter, which was fine with Dana. So when they'd dated, they'd stuck pretty close to the ranch or else they'd gone out for a hamburger and a movie. At that same time, Kieran had been working on a special project for Robinson Tech, so Dana had only run into him a couple of times.

Still, his comment and his curiosity took her aback. She wasn't here to make any kind of personal connection with him. Sure, she sympathized with him and wanted to offer her help with Rosie. But this visit wasn't about her.

"There's not much to tell," she said. "I'm in grad school, although I took a break from my classes this semester to focus on a special project for the Austin History Center. I work there as a researcher."

"I knew that much," he said. "What do you do on your days off?"

She didn't usually share that sort of thing with people her age, since her favorite things to do might be considered unusual. But she decided there wasn't any reason to worry about what Kieran might think. "I enjoy taking long walks in my neighborhood, shopping in my favorite antiques store and going to estate sales."

"Seriously?"

See? He was no different from anyone else.

"Yes," she admitted. "I bought a house in Hyde Park and like to find interesting things to decorate it the way it might have looked back in 1948, when it was built."

He studied her a moment, as if still trying to decide whether she was pulling his leg, then smiled. "I'd like to see your place someday."

Now she was the one to wonder if he was being sincere or just being polite and making small talk. But she shrugged it off and said, "I'd be happy to show it to you. I'm proud of the way it's all coming together."

"Do you own the house?" he asked. "Or are you renting?"

Was he wondering if she could afford to buy a place of her own?

She supposed he'd have no reason to ask, other than plain curiosity, so she leveled with him. "I purchased a two-bedroom fixer-upper about six months ago with the idea of flipping it, but the renovations took a while and were a lot of work. So now that it's done, I'd like to enjoy the fruits of my labor for a while."

"Are you going to keep it, then?"

"No, within the next six months, I'll sell it and buy another in the same neighborhood."

He took another drink of beer and eyed her carefully. "I'm impressed."

With *her*?

Or with the completed renovation project?

"Now I'd really like to see it," he added.

Okay, so it had been the work she'd done on the house that had surprised and intrigued him.

"You're more than welcome to stop by anytime," she said. "It's not as classy, modern or impressive as your place, but it's warm and appealing to me." And to be honest, even though she'd never admit it to anyone else, she was also proud of the house since she'd done most of the work herself.

"Why doesn't that surprise me?" he asked, a smile lighting his blue eyes.

She'd never been especially comfortable talking about herself or blowing her own horn, so she steered the conversation back to a topic that would suit them both better. "I hope you'll bring Rosie when you come."

"Of course."

"And speaking of Rosie, have you hired a nanny or housekeeper yet?"

"No, and I'd rather not—if I don't have to. She attends preschool three days a week, so I'll go to the office then. And on Tuesdays and Thursdays, I'll work from home."

"That sounds like a good plan."

"I hope so." He glanced past her, his gaze landing on the toys, dolls and games cluttering the living area. "But I'm probably going to need my cleaning lady to come more often than once a week. Who would have guessed a child could wreak so much havoc?"

As wild and wacky as she'd found Kieran's over-zealous attempt to provide for little Rosie, her heart went out to the poor man.

"You know," she said, "I was serious when I offered to help out whenever I can."

"Don't be surprised when I take you up on that offer." He flashed a dazzling smile that set off a flutter in her tummy again. But this time, the bevy of butterflies wasn't caused by nervousness. Instead, it was due to sheer anticipation.

Too bad she couldn't take back her offer to assist him with Rosie. Even the slightest thought of striking up a friendship—let alone a romance—with a man like Kieran Fortune was out of line.

And bound to end in disappointment.

Working from home two days a week wasn't the best situation, but as the vice president of Robinson Tech, Kieran could make his own schedule, so it was certainly doable. Besides, he'd promised Zach he would take care of his little girl, and he wasn't about to farm out the job.

Unfortunately, his work-from-home plan didn't last long. Being productive while having a preschooler underfoot was next to impossible. For some reason, he'd thought that Rosie would be able to play quietly and entertain herself, but he'd been wrong about that.

He'd also thought that, after practically buying out the toy section at Kids' World, she'd have enough to keep her busy until kindergarten. But that wasn't the case, either.

She might start out working on a puzzle or skimming the pictures in a book, but she got bored easily and wanted him to play with her. He'd put her off as often as he could, but before he knew it, he was the one doing the entertaining. The only time she sat still and let him work without interruption was when he put on a DVD for her, but he couldn't very well do that from morning until night.

Now, as he prepared a spreadsheet for tomorrow's board meeting, she again walked up to him and tugged on his sleeve. "Uncle Kieran?"

"Yes, honey?" He tore his gaze from the sales numbers and looked at the cute little imp, who held a toy medical bag in her hand.

Early this morning, he'd combed her hair and pulled her blond locks into an uneven and messy ponytail. But no matter how hard he'd tried, he hadn't been able to get the rubber band on evenly. And the red bow she'd insisted on wearing only served to point out how lopsided it was. Still, she was a cute kid, with big green eyes and thick dark lashes.

"Will you play with me?" she asked. "I'll be the doctor, and you can be sick."

"I'm pretty busy right now," he said. "Can't you find something else to do?"

Her lips curled into a pout, then she brightened. "I could make pizza and hamburgers for your dinner."

"That sounds great." Especially if her return to the

play kitchen in the living room would buy him another few minutes to finish his spreadsheet.

As she scampered off, he glanced at the time on his laptop. Weren't kids supposed to take afternoon naps? Dana said they did, but it looked as if Rosie hadn't gotten that memo.

As much as Kieran wanted to handle things on his own, he realized that wasn't going to work. His first thought was to ask one of his brothers or sisters to help out, but Rosie would probably be more comfortable with a woman.

The only problem was, Rachel lived in Horseback Hollow. Zoe was in charge of brand management for Robinson Computers, overseeing the company's presence on social media, plus organizing events to raise the company's profile. And if that wasn't enough to keep her occupied, she was happily married to Joaquin Mendoza, who took up any free time she might have.

Sophie worked as an assistant HR director at Robinson Tech, which kept her busy. She was also all starry-eyed these days, thanks to her recent engagement to Mason Montgomery. And Olivia, who was still single, was a computer programmer at the company. Clearly, his sisters all had lives of their own, so he couldn't ask any of them.

And even if they did have the time, they'd all been a little skeptical of his ability to be a father. So there was no way he'd reveal that he was struggling. Instead, he'd prove them wrong, even if it killed him.

At the sound of the battery-operated motor of the little car, Kieran swore under his breath. If Rosie ran it into the dining room table leg one more time…

Oh, hell. Why wait until then? As soon as she took a nap—if she ever did—he'd call the doorman and ask him to get rid of it, even if that meant putting it out on the curb with a sign saying: Free to a Good Home.

A loud thump sounded from the dining area, which meant Rosie had crashed into the table again. What in the world made him think he could handle child rearing on his own?

I'll help any way I can, Dana had said. And she'd seemed sincere.

Kieran whipped out his cell phone, ready to call her right now and take her up on that offer.

Of all the places Dana could have imagined having dinner on a Tuesday evening, Cowboy Fred's Funhouse and Pizza Emporium wasn't one of them. But when Kieran called to invite her to join him and Rosie for an early dinner, he'd sounded a little frazzled. And when he'd admitted that he wanted an adult to talk to, she'd agreed. Then she'd hurried home to shut off her Crock-Pot, in which she'd placed a small roast before leaving for work this morning. Once she'd placed the meat in the fridge, she'd changed her clothes.

She'd been a little flattered by Kieran's invitation until she realized there was no way he'd ever want to meet a date at one of the most popular kids' eateries in Austin. Still, she'd applied lipstick and hurried to meet him.

She found him standing out in front of Cowboy Fred's, holding Rosie's hand. He was dressed more casually than usual in a pair of black jeans and a maroon-and-white golf shirt bearing a Texas A&M logo.

When Rosie, who wore a pair of pink shorts and a white T-shirt with a princess graphic, spotted Dana, she burst into a happy grin and squealed, "Dannnnnnna!"

The girl's happy reaction was heartwarming, but it was Kieran's dazzling smile that set Dana's pulse soaring at a wacky rate.

"Thanks for joining us," he said, as he greeted Dana in front of the bright red door encircled with blinking theater lights. "I owe you."

She winked at him, then studied little Rosie's lopsided ponytail, the red ribbon dangling unevenly and about to slide off.

"We've been cooped up all day," Kieran said, "so we both needed to get out. But next time, we'll invite you to have grilled steaks at my house."

Next time? So he'd be calling her again and asking her to join him, only next time at his place?

Now, that was an interesting thought.

He grabbed the brass handle and opened the red door for her and Rosie to enter. When the child dashed inside and waited for a greeter dressed in a cowboy costume to stamp her hand, Dana followed, dazed by the rows of mechanical ponies and cars, by the huge room filled with video games.

The flashing lights and the electronic bleeps made her think of a kiddie casino. Wow. This place was wild. And *loud*. Now she knew what Kieran meant about "owing her."

"Ma'am," the cowboy said, "I'll need to stamp your hand, too. Yours, too, sir. Each child's number needs to match the adults' who brought her."

"Uncle Kieran," Rosie asked, "can I please go play on the climb-y thing?"

"Sure, princess. You go ahead." He pointed to a blue bench that was stationed close to the structure. "As soon as we get our hands stamped, Dana and I will be sitting right there, waiting for you."

As the happy girl hurried off, Kieran turned to Dana and asked, "Can you believe this place?"

"I'd heard about it from a coworker who has a boy in kindergarten, but I'm a little surprised by the lights and noise. I'd think that would cause sensory overload for the kids. I wonder if any of them actually take time to sit down and eat."

Kieran laughed. "Maybe not, but I see a couple of dads ordering a beer near that sign that says Chuck Wagon. I think I'll follow their lead. Would you like something to drink, too?"

"I'll have a glass of wine—if they have it. Thanks."

While Kieran went to the counter, Dana made her way to the blue bench and took a seat. Moments later, he returned with his beer and her wine, both served in clear plastic glasses. "I'm afraid I'm going to owe you a better vintage when you come to my house."

So he hadn't been just blowing smoke about inviting her to his place for dinner. Not that she'd sensed anything romantic about it.

"How about Thursday?" he asked. "I'm not going into the office that day."

She rarely made evening plans during the week, so she didn't need to check her calendar. "Sure, that's fine." She studied the man seated beside her, the way he seemed comfortable in his skin, even at a place like Cowboy Fred's.

"You told me you were going to work from home a couple days a week," she said. "How's that going?"

"Not as well as I'd hoped. I haven't been able to get much done, so I end up staying at the office longer on the days Rosie's in preschool. Only trouble is, I have to pick her up before six o'clock, and when I finally arrived yesterday, she was the last kid there. She didn't seem unhappy about it, but I felt bad."

"I can understand that, but I'll bet things will begin to run smoothly soon. And then you'll fall into the perfect schedule."

He stretched his arm out along the back of the bench, his hand dangling close to her shoulder. Close enough to touch, actually.

"Thanks for your vote of confidence," he said, "but I have to admit I'm not so sure that'll ever happen."

She took a sip of the wine, something cheap and most likely out of a box. Not that she was a connoisseur by any means, but she didn't mind paying a little more for something decent.

"I have a favor to ask," he said. "Remember when you offered to help me out?"

"Yes, and I meant it." She adored Rosie and was

glad to play a role in her life. She also sympathized with Kieran, although she wondered if what she was feeling for him might be a little more than that. Still, she had no misconceptions about ever developing anything other than a friendship with the gorgeous and brilliant executive. But he clearly needed help, and he was asking for hers.

"I don't know anything about kids or child rearing," he said.

Neither did Dana, for that matter, but she planned to read some parenting books and articles so she'd have more to offer him than a respite now and then.

"What's on your mind?" she asked.

"That's just it. I'm not sure. My childhood wasn't typical, and I don't just mean because I grew up in a wealthy family. I was practically raised by nannies—and none of them stuck around very long."

"I'm afraid mine wasn't that much better," Dana said. "I lost both my parents in an accident, then I spent my teen years in foster care."

At that admission, Kieran turned in his seat, his knee pressing into hers and zapping her with a jolt of heat. His gaze latched on to hers, as if he'd felt it, too. But surely he hadn't.

"I'm sorry," he said. "I hope it didn't sound as if I was complaining about my lot in life, when yours…"

"I survived. And for the record, my time in foster care wasn't what you'd call a bad experience. I could have had it a lot worse."

When he didn't respond, she feared she'd put a

damper on things, so she smiled and said, "On the upside, my foster family lived next door to the public library, where I liked to hang out. I passed the time by reading all the books I could get my hands on, especially those in the history section. That's also where I did my homework, met my best friend, learned to do research and then created my career plan. So it all paid off in the long run."

"Now I understand why you work at the history center."

He probably found that incredibly boring, but she wasn't about to stretch the truth and make herself sound like someone he'd be more interested in. *Interested in for what?* she asked herself. Dating came to mind, but that wasn't going to happen, so she halted that line of thinking. She continued to tell him her life story as dull as he might find it.

"Once I turned eighteen," she said, "I was on my own. I was a good student, and a young librarian named Monica Flores convinced me that an education was the key to a successful life, so I went to college." She also graduated with honors, but decided not to mention it. She did, however add, "I'm not in school this semester, but I'm going to pick up a class this summer and two more in the fall. If all goes as planned, I'll have a master's degree in history by mid-December."

"You're a busy lady."

She offered him a shy but warm smile. "Not too busy for you and Rosie."

Again their gazes met and locked. That is, until Rosie yelled, "Dannnna!"

They both looked up to see the little girl in the yellow tunnel of the climbing structure. She waved at them through a plastic window.

Dana waved back. "We see you, sweetie."

"Are you hungry yet?" Kieran called out.

"No!" Rosie shrieked before crawling onto another section of the structure, one that housed a red slide.

"It might take a while for them to make the pizza," Kieran said. "I'd better order it now. I found out the hard way that Rosie goes from not being the least bit hungry to starving in the blink of an eye."

He'd no more than gotten to his feet when Rosie screamed. At least, it sounded like her cry and came from the direction she'd been heading.

They both jumped up and hurried to the far side of the structure where Rosie sat on a pad at the bottom of the slide. She was crying, the lower half of her face covered in blood.

"Oh, my God," Dana said, as she hurried to the injured child. "What happened, sweetie?"

"A bad boy punched my nose!" she shrieked.

Dana shot a glance at Kieran, who'd come up beside her. He'd paled at the sight of little Rosie, yet he scanned the structure as if looking for the boy.

"Come with me," Dana said, scooping up the bloodied child in her arms. "Let's get you cleaned up."

"Where's the kid who hurt you?" Kieran asked Rosie.

She pointed to the top of the slide. "He's the one. In the green shirt with a dragon."

Dana didn't see anyone there and assumed the boy had run away. But Kieran must have because he took off like a bolt, obviously in search of the boy who'd hurt his little princess.

Chapter Four

Kieran wasn't sure where the "bad boy" had gone, but he was determined to find him. What kind of hellion would bloody a little girl's nose?

Righteous indignation grew into flat-out anger with each step he took in his search. Not only would he confront the kid who'd hurt Rosie, but he was going to have a little talk with the mom and dad, too.

When he spotted the only boy wearing a green dragon shirt in the vicinity, he realized the bully was much smaller than he'd thought. In fact, he didn't appear to be any older than Rosie.

Before Kieran could take another step, the boy's mother swooped in and, from the crease in her forehead, the frown on her lips and the grip on his arm, she appeared to be well aware of what he'd done.

Kieran slowed to a stop. As he stood off to the side, close enough to hear the conversation, he observed the parent and child.

"What happened?" the mom asked the boy. "Did you *hit* that little girl?"

"Yes. But she punched me first!" He pointed to his eye, which appeared to be a little red. "Right here! And it *still* hurts."

The mother dropped to one knee and studied the alleged injury carefully. "Why did she do that?"

"I don't know." He grimaced. "I told her my dragon likes to eat princesses, and I told her she better get out of the way. Then she did this." He fisted his small hand and made a punching motion toward his eye.

"I'm sorry she hurt you, but that didn't mean you had the right to hit her back. You're going to have to tell her you're sorry."

The boy looked down at his scuffed sneakers then back at his mom with a frown. "Okay. But she has to say sorry, too."

"I'm not worried about her manners. I'm concerned about yours. You know better than to hurt someone, even if they hit you first."

His chin dropped to his chest, resting on the graphic, right about where a burst of fire came out of the dragon's mouth. "Okay. But will you come with me?"

"Yes, I will."

As the mother bent forward and placed a kiss on her son's cheek, Kieran realized he didn't need to get involved after all. The woman clearly loved the boy and was teaching him right from wrong, as well as showing him how to be kind and thoughtful. So he turned and walked away.

He wished he'd had a parent like that when he'd been growing up. Not that he hadn't been loved or disciplined, but more often than not, those lessons had come from nannies and au pairs—and minus the kiss on the cheek.

When he reached the big red slide, Dana still wasn't back from the restroom where she'd taken Rosie to wash off the blood. He hadn't liked seeing Rosie hurt, but she'd probably learned a hard and painful lesson.

Hopefully, she hadn't been seriously injured. When he'd been a boy, he'd gotten a couple of bloody noses, and he had never suffered any lasting damage.

But that didn't make this any easier. When he'd heard Rosie cry, when he'd seen the blood dribbling from her nose, his heart had dropped to the floor, and he'd almost lost it. All he could think about was chasing after that bully and making sure he didn't get away with hitting a little girl. But that was before he'd found out that the princess had struck the dragon first.

Now what? What would a real father do at a time like this?

Too bad he didn't have any memories to draw from so he could teach by example. His dad had been a workaholic, and by the time Kieran had come around, Gerald Robinson practically lived at the office or was flying off to who knew where.

And his mom hadn't been around much, either. She'd been too caught up in shopping trips to Manhattan, visits to spas and hair salons and whatever else it was some mothers did when they didn't have time for their kids.

Still, he was going to have to talk to Rosie, just as the boy's mom had done with him.

How would Zach have handled this?

Too bad Kieran couldn't just whip out his cell phone and ask.

No, he was on his own from now on, and his gut clenched at the thought.

That is, until Dana walked out of the bathroom, a reminder that he wasn't entirely alone. She still held Rosie in her arms. The new princess shirt he'd bought her was now bloodstained and probably ruined. So was Dana's lacy blouse.

On the upside, it appeared that the bleeding had stopped.

"How's she doing?" Kieran asked.

"She's all right. Just a little sore." Dana brushed a motherly kiss on Rosie's brow. It was a sweet move, a touching one.

Had Zach lived, Dana probably would have filled a maternal role in the child's life.

"Hey," Kieran said to Rosie. "You and I are going to have to go find that boy so you can apologize to him."

Dana didn't object, but she scrunched her brow, clearly confused by Kieran's comment.

"Apparently," he said, filling her in, "Rosie struck the first blow." Then he turned back to Rosie, "Of course, two wrongs don't make a right. And hitting hurts. That's why we don't punch people when we get mad."

"No." Rosie crossed her arms in an unexpected show of defiance. "I'm *not* gonna say sorry to him."

Kieran looked at Dana, hoping she'd help him figure out the proper approach.

She gave a slight shrug, then turned Rosie to face her. "When we hurt someone, we apologize. It's the right thing to do."

Rosie scrunched her little face. "Do I have to?"

"Yes, you do," Dana said.

"I'll go with you," Kieran offered, just as the boy's mom had done.

Rosie rolled her eyes. "Okay, but then I want to go home."

Now she was talking. Kieran had already spent more time at Cowboy Fred's than he wanted to. "I've got an even better idea, Rosie. I'll ask the guy at the counter to box up our pizza so we can take it with us. What do you say about that?"

"Okay," she said. "Can we eat it and watch a princess movie on TV?"

"Absolutely. Now come on, let's go face that dragon."

Moments later, they found the boy standing next to his mother, scanning the climbing structure and probably looking for Rosie. Dana placed the girl on the floor, and Kieran took her hand in his, but he had to give it a little tug to get her to move forward and face the boy and his mom.

"I'm sorry for punching you," she told the child.

The boy looked at Rosie. "I'm sorry, too. I didn't mean to make blood come out of your nose."

"Tell her your name," the boy's mother suggested. "That way, maybe you can be friends and play together."

The boy didn't say a word, and Rosie merely stared at him.

The mother placed her hand on her son's head. "This is Michael."

"Yeah," he said, directing his response to Rosie. "But sometimes people call me Indiana Jones, 'specially when I have my toy whip."

Rosie smiled. "Then you can call me Princess Rosabelle." She must have thought of something because her smile faded. "I'm not going to play with you when you have a whip."

Michael shrugged, then turned to his mother and wrapped his arms around her leg, clearly glad the apology was over.

Apparently so was Rosie because she hurried back to Dana and lifted her arms, making it known that she wanted to be picked up again.

When Dana complied, Rosie hugged her neck. "Let's go home now, Uncle Kieran."

"Maybe," Michael's mom said, "the next time you come to Cowboy Fred's, we'll be here, too. And then you and Michael can play together."

Kieran didn't know about that, but he offered the mom a smile. Then he went to the counter and told the teenage clerk to make their order to go.

"Perfect timing," the teen said. "Your pizza is just coming out of the oven."

Moments later, with the large pizza box in hand, Kieran found Dana and Rosie at the entrance, having the matching stamps on their hands verified.

"Why don't you follow us back to my place?" he suggested. "I promised you pizza for dinner, and I don't want you to think I'd ever renege on a deal like that."

Her pretty smile lit her eyes, reminding him of a field of bluebonnets.

"Sure, why not?"

When she shifted Rosie in her arms, he again spotted the blood splatter on her blouse. "Looks like I'm going to owe you a new top."

"Don't worry about it."

"I insist."

She shook her head. "Actually, you'd never be able to find another like this. I bought it at a vintage clothing shop downtown, so it's one of a kind."

If it was that rare, it was probably also expensive. "Now I really feel bad."

"Don't," she said, as she pushed open the door. "Believe it or not, I'm up on all the latest techniques for stain removal. I learned them because of the unique places I sometimes shop."

"You like to wear vintage clothing?"

"Yes. I actually prefer it."

At that, his steps slowed. Hers did, too. When their eyes met, he studied her for a moment. Dana was a novelty and one of a kind, just like her favorite articles of clothing.

With unabashed honesty, he said, "I've never met anyone like you."

He'd expected her to brighten, to take his flattering remark to heart, like most of the women he knew would have done. But her waifish smile made him wonder if she'd taken his comment differently than he'd actually meant it.

"I'm sure you haven't," she said, her voice soft and vulnerable—maybe even hurt.

"That was actually a compliment," he told her.

"Then thank you." She smiled again, and while it seemed a lot more genuine this time, her eyes weren't nearly as bright.

If she were another woman, one of those he usually dated, he'd apologize by surprising her with a piece of jewelry or by taking her someplace special.

But Dana didn't seem to be the kind of woman to get caught up in high-priced trappings. And, while that left him without a ready peace offering, it pleased him in an unexpected way.

Dana had to admit that an evening spent watching animated movies while eating pizza never had sounded appealing, at least not since she'd graduated from high school. But on the drive over to Kieran's condominium, she'd actually looked forward to having dinner with him and Rosie.

Now, as they sat on the floor, around a modern, glass-topped coffee table and watching a classic cartoon movie on television, she found herself having fun. Rosie was an absolute delight and said some of the cutest things. Her happy chatter had both adults smiling more often than not.

Dana's only complaint, if you could call it that, was the meal itself. Cowboy Fred's pizza was the worst she'd ever eaten. No, she'd have to take that back. When she was a teenager, her foster dad used to stop by a sports bar on his way home from work on Friday nights. He'd meet his wife there so they could have a couple of beers with their friends. After they'd "wound down" from a stressful workweek, they would bring home cold pizza for Dana and the other kids to eat. The topping was always greasy, the crust tough and hard to chew. Looking back, she suspected that, even if they'd brought it straight home still warm from the oven, it wouldn't have tasted any better.

Rosie reached for her glass and downed the last of her milk. "I'm all done." Then she pushed her plate aside and zeroed in on the movie.

Kieran, who sat next to Dana, turned to her and asked, "Do you think she had enough to eat? She ate the cheese off the top, but she only took a couple of bites of the crust."

Dana offered him a slight shrug. "Who knows? At least she drank her milk."

"Is that enough to hold her over until breakfast?" Kieran asked.

"It might be."

Dana had to force herself to finish her own single slice, but she didn't mention that to Kieran. She'd hate for him to think she was complaining about the meal he'd provided her.

"Actually," he said, "I've been known to eat almost an entire pizza by myself, but this one tastes like *C-R-A-P.*"

At that, Dana broke into a grin. "That might be one reason she didn't finish. Should we offer her something else? If you have some fresh fruit or yogurt, we can tempt her with something more appealing."

"Good idea," he said. "You stay here, kick back and relax. I'll see what I can rustle up."

The children's movie wasn't all that bad. In fact, it was somewhat entertaining, but Dana got to her feet anyway. "Let me help."

"Are you sure you want to?"

She gave him a wink. "You bet."

Several minutes later, they'd prepared a fruit, cheese and cracker platter.

"Maybe I'd better spread some peanut butter on a few of these crackers," Kieran said. "Earlier today, during lunch, Rosie informed me that mouse cheese tastes yucky and that she only likes the square kind."

Dana tilted her head. "What did she mean by that?"

"I wondered the same thing, so I asked." Kieran laughed. "She said the cartoon mice eat cheese that has holes in it. So I came to an easy conclusion. She prefers American over Swiss."

"Well, what do you know? There's something new to learn every day."

"That's true, especially when there's a three-year-old around. But I catch on quickly. Now I have American cheese on my new grocery list, along with raisins and Oreos, although she informed me she only likes the 'white stuff inside' and not the cookie part."

"That's important to note," Dana said, as she finished slicing an apple to add to the platter, which was now filled with healthy munchies and adorned with both green and red grapes. "What do you think? Is this enough?"

Kieran made his way to where she stood, close enough for her to catch a taunting whiff of his woodsy aftershave. "That's perfect. We make a great team."

Did they? She liked the sound of that.

"And after the day we've had," he added, giving her a nudge with his elbow, "and the movie we're committed to finish, I'd like to have a glass of wine. How about you? I promise it'll come out of a bottle, rather than a box."

"That sounds good to me."

She watched as he opened the stainless-steel refrigerator door, pulled out a chilled chardonnay and placed it on the countertop. She again marveled at the way he moved through the kitchen, like a man comfortable being a host. Or, more accurately, like a bachelor who'd perfected the fine art of seduction.

And why wouldn't a rich, handsome single man-like Kieran have those romantic moves down to a science?

Of course, giving Dana a glass of wine after an evening like this wasn't about romance or seduction. Still, if she were to ever be on the receiving end of Kieran Fortune's sexual attention, she'd be charmed to the core. And making love with him would be as natural as…falling into bed.

Now there was an amazing and completely unlikely image she wasn't going to dwell on.

After opening the bottle with a fancy corkscrew, Kieran removed two crystal goblets from the glass-door cupboard and filled them halfway.

He handed one to Dana, then lifted his in a toast. "To my trusty teammate, who happens to be a very good sport."

Her heart fluttered, as if they had actually become a team, but that's as far as it would go. She knew better than to let anything Kieran said go to her head. So she tamped down the little rush, determined to offer him a lighthearted toast of her own.

She clinked her glass against his, the resonating ring validating the glasses were crystal, and said, "To Cowboy Fred's search for a new chef."

At that, Kieran chuckled. "You've got that right. And to make matters worse, there's a great Italian restaurant close to my office that serves an awesome gourmet pizza—and for less than Fred charges for week-old marinara and stale cheese on top of baked cardboard."

Now it was Dana's turn to laugh. Then she reached for a grape, pulled it off the small cluster and popped it into her mouth.

"Come on," Kieran said. "Let's take this to Rosie and give her something healthier to eat for dinner."

They'd no more than returned to the living room

when they spotted Rosie stretched out on the floor, her eyes closed in slumber, her lips parted.

"Is she asleep?" Dana asked.

"It looks that way." Kieran set both his wineglass and the platter on the coffee table. "She should eat something, but…she's got to be exhausted. Maybe it would be best to let her sleep. If she wakes up hungry, I can give her something to eat then."

He stooped and picked up the child, then straightened, holding her close to his chest, gazing at her as if she was a fragile princess. She might be tiny and precious, but she'd battled a dragon today.

"I'll be right back," Kieran said. Then he carried Rosie out of the living room and down the hall.

Dana glanced at the platter of cheese and fruit as well as Kieran's glass of wine. Then she looked at her own. A nervous flutter erupted in her tummy.

With Rosie now out of the room, they would be alone. What in the world would they talk about?

That romantic spark she'd felt while bumping elbows with him in the kitchen flickered again, warming her cheeks and sending her heart in a tail-chasing circle. She tried her best to put the fire out, to tamp it down, just as she'd done before.

But this time, watching Kieran walk away, all tall, buff and handsome, his sexy swagger on, she just couldn't shake whatever he'd stirred inside her.

When Kieran returned to the living room, he found Dana seated on the sofa, rather than on the floor where they'd sat before. That made sense. There was no point in having a big, family-style evening when Rosie was sound asleep.

He looked at his new Bang & Olufsen television screen, where the animated movie continued to play, and reached for the remote, which rested on the lamp table. "I assume it's okay if I turn this off."

"That's fine by me." Dana offered him a shy smile, then studied the wine in her crystal goblet as if she'd never seen anything like it before.

He felt a little awkward, too. But he shook it off and took a seat on the sofa, one cushion away from her. Then he picked up his wineglass, which he'd left on the coffee table just moments ago. "It looks like we'll have the food to ourselves."

Dana bent forward and snatched a piece of cheese and a rice cracker from the platter. As she did, the lamplight splashed on her bent head in such a way that it lit up threads of gold in her auburn strands, causing her silky hair to shimmer and glisten like it was about to catch fire. He could only imagine what it would look like if she wore it hanging loose.

Kieran hadn't expected to notice something like that, let alone comment, but a question rolled off his tongue before he could give it a second thought. "Is there a reason you keep your hair pulled up most of the time?"

Dana gazed up at him, the cheese and cracker half raised to her mouth. Her lips parted as if the question had completely caught her off guard. But then, why wouldn't it take her aback? Kieran hadn't intended to ask her something so personal, even if he'd wondered about it more than once in the last few weeks.

"It's just a habit, I guess. I always put it up when I'm at work because it tends to get into my face whenever I'm bent over a book or a journal. But I…" She didn't finish what she was about to add.

The way she eyed him, carefully and cautiously, made him scamper to find an excuse or an explanation for asking such a question in the first place.

"It's a pretty color," he admitted, "and I'd think…" Oh, for cripe's sake. *Good job, man. Now you've made things worse.*

Where did he go from here? If she were a classy, beautiful woman seated alone in a swanky bar, sipping champagne and wearing a coquettish grin, he'd have no trouble knowing just what to do and say right now. And he wouldn't even consider changing the subject. But this was different.

Dana was different.

And in her own way, even with her hair pulled up and dressed in casual clothes, she seemed just as appealing as any woman he might meet in a bar. In fact, if she would consider letting her hair down and slipping into a slinky black dress…

Oh, hell. She didn't even need to go to that length. As it was, he found her pretty damn intriguing.

And there lay the crux of the problem. Under other circumstances, Kieran would have made a romantic move by now. But he couldn't very well do that when she'd been Zach's girlfriend. Guys didn't do things like that to each other.

"Is something wrong?" she asked.

Hell, yes. Even with her hair pulled up like a prim librarian and with a blood stain on her blouse, she'd caught his eye and his full attention. And he found her way more attractive than he should.

"No," he said, doing his damnedest to shake the sudden attraction and to pull himself together. "There's nothing wrong. My mind was just wandering back in time, back to when Zach was alive. The two of you came to a cocktail party here. And you wore your hair down that evening. It hung nearly to your waist and was so sleek and shiny. The color was even more striking. I didn't tell you then, but I commented about it later to Zach."

"He liked me to wear it long and loose, but…" She bit down on her bottom lip, as if trying to hold back whatever she'd been about to say.

But that was okay. In fact, it was almost a relief to know they'd both gotten caught up in a topic that needed to be redirected—and quickly. If he didn't get off this verbal merry-go-round, he could end up saying something really stupid, something that gave Dana the wrong idea.

"Unlike Zach," he said, grasping at straws, "I've always been attracted to blondes."

The second the words rolled off his tongue, heat flooded his face, and his breathing stopped.

How was that for failing miserably in his attempt to fix things?

Trying to recover, he added, "But I *do* like the color and think you should wear it down more often."

Oh, hell. Great recovery. That thoughtless attempt just threw him back into the quagmire he'd tried to escape.

"Thank you," she said. Then she reached for her glass and took another sip of wine.

So no harm, no foul?

Hopefully, they were back on the right track. He wasn't about to put the moves on his late friend's girlfriend, especially when he desperately needed her friendship.

He'd only screw things up by revealing his attraction to her. Besides, sexual partners were a dime a dozen as far as Kieran was concerned.

Yet for some reason, at least tonight, Dana appeared to be one in a million.

Chapter Five

Dana had no idea what Kieran meant by first complimenting her, then slamming her with the fact that he preferred blondes over redheads.

She'd been so dazed by his first comment that she'd caught her breath. She'd almost believed that he found her pretty, and she could have sworn that something sparked between them. She'd inadvertently lifted her hand and fingered the neatly woven strands.

Then, just when she'd thought he was going to say something romantic, he seemed to have realized his error. His smile faded, and his expression froze, making him look like a deer in the headlights. Or in this case, a bachelor in the headlights. He quickly recovered, although awkwardly, and changed the subject.

Apparently her initial instinct had been wrong. He

hadn't meant to lead her to believe he was actually interested in her, and she felt like a fool.

But what did she know about men like Kieran? Other than Zach, who'd felt more like a friend than a date, she'd only had one real boyfriend, and that relationship hadn't lasted very long.

It had taken a few years of college for her to shed her teenage insecurities, something she blamed on losing her parents so young and being a foster kid. But now she celebrated the fact that she was unique and valuable in her own right, something Monica Flores, the young librarian who'd befriended her, had helped her see. And she wasn't about to slip back into those old, bad habits again.

In an attempt to take control of her tender feelings, she reached for her wineglass, pretending to be completely unaffected by anything Kieran had said. But instead of taking a ladylike sip, she took a rather large gulp, choked and sputtered.

"Are you okay?" he asked.

Talk about uncomfortable moments. "Yes." She covered her mouth and coughed several times. "I'm… fine."

And she was. Kieran was probably afraid that Dana had taken his comment wrong. And maybe she had, but only for a moment. She knew better than to imagine he'd meant anything flirtatious.

Over the years, she'd gotten a lot of compliments on her hair. When she was a little girl, whether at the market or shopping in a department store with her mother, people would stop them all the time and comment about the color. Of course, most of them had been sweet, little old ladies. So her ego hadn't taken that big of a hit now. At least, not one that would be lasting.

Actually, she almost felt sorry for Kieran. He might be uneasy because of what he'd said and afraid of how she might have taken it. But she hadn't gotten the wrong idea. There was no way she'd ever assume that she could just waltz right into his world and easily fit in with the women who ran in his crowd.

"You know," she said, getting to her feet, "I've got to get going. I just realized I put something in my Crock-Pot early this morning."

It was the truth. Well, in a way, it was. He didn't have to know she'd already taken it out.

"I'm sorry if I made you uneasy," he said, rising quickly. "You really do have beautiful hair and probably should wear it down more often. But I don't want you to think I was hitting on you. I only mentioned my attraction to blondes because... Well, it was completely out of line. And it wasn't true."

She laughed, hoping her attempt to feign an unaffected, don't-give-it-a-second-thought attitude sounded real to him and not canned. "I knew you weren't being flirtatious."

At that, his expression softened, and his posture eased. "Good, because I'd really like your help with Rosie, and I'd hate to think you might feel uncomfortable around me."

So there you had it. He needed her to be a part of Team Rosie and nothing more. Dana was fine with that. Really. After all, Zach's little girl and her well-

being were all that mattered. And Dana had never
expected her and Kieran to be anything other than
friends.

Still, as she gathered her purse and headed for the
door, a wave of disappointment swept over her, threatening to flood every step she took.

Dana and Kieran hadn't talked since their last awkward evening, although there was more than one reason for that. She'd been especially busy at the history
center for the past couple of days, working on a special
project she didn't wrap up until Friday afternoon. Then
she'd met Connie and Alisha, two of her coworkers, for
happy hour, followed by dinner. She hadn't discussed
Kieran with them because, while she considered them
friends, she wouldn't call them confidantes.

Finally, on Saturday morning, she decided she'd
bottled up her feelings for too long. So while having a
cup of English breakfast tea and a toasted bagel with
cream cheese, she called Monica, who still lived in
Amarillo and worked at the library.

Monica was everything Dana wasn't—spunky,
beautiful, stylish and petite. She also had a flawless
olive complexion, expressive brown eyes and glossy,
dark hair she often wore as a mass of riotous curls
that bounced along her shoulders and onto her back.

At thirty-one, and six years older than Dana, Monica had easily slid into a mentor role. And before long,
the two had grown incredibly close, best friends to
be sure. But Monica had become the big sister Dana
never had. She was also the only one in the world

who understood the relationship Dana had shared with Zach, his daughter and his parents.

"Hey, girl!" Monica said. "How's it going? Are you holding up okay?"

"I'm doing well. How about you?"

"There've been a few changes since we last talked. Sergio and I decided to call it quits."

"I'm sorry to hear that."

"Me, too. But it was a mutual decision, and it's for the best. Most of our time was spent arguing, and I'm tired of it. I'd rather have a peaceful life."

"So what else is new?" Dana asked.

"My *abuelita* moved in with my parents. She's been doing the cooking, so I've been going home a lot, just to eat. And now I've put on about five pounds."

"I can understand why. Your grandmother is an awesome cook." Dana laughed and her spirits rose. She needed to talk to Monica more often than she did. "I really miss the time I used to spend at your parents' house. How are they?"

"Working their tails off. Business at their floral shop seems to have really taken off, so that's good."

Dana bit down on her bottom lip. She'd never held back when sharing her thoughts, fears or dreams with Monica, but how should she word her current dilemma when she didn't quite understand it herself?

She decided to start with the basics. "Zach's best friend, Kieran Fortune, has custody of Rosie. So I've been helping him when I can."

Silence stretched across the line for a couple of beats, then Monica, who'd apparently picked up on something in Dana's tone, prodded her for more details. "And...?"

"It's nothing, really. I just... Well, things are getting a little weird because, as much as I adore Rosie and want to help, Kieran is...well, he's handsome, successful and ultrawealthy. He's also so far out of my league that I'd never fit in with his family or friends if I tried. And on top of that, he'd never be interested in someone like me anyway."

"Awww..."

"What's that supposed to mean?"

"Don't doubt yourself, *chica*. You're brighter and far more beautiful than you've ever realized. And you have plenty to offer a man like that—particularly a loving and loyal heart."

Dana rolled her eyes. "Have you ever heard of Robinson Tech or the Fortune Foundation?"

There was another pause, then a long, drawn out whistle. "You mean he's *that* Kieran Fortune, as in Kieran Fortune Robinson? You mentioned the last name, but since he and Zach were friends, I didn't make the connection. I mean, Zach was a rancher."

"They met at college. Played football together, if I remember correctly and were in the same fraternity. Plus, believe it or not, Zach was pretty sharp. People didn't always recognize that since he tended to speak slowly and with a Texas twang."

"Still," Monica said, "I repeat—you're bright, beautiful and have a loving and loyal heart. You have a lot to offer any man, even one from a wealthy, renowned family."

"Intellectually I know that."

Monica clicked her tongue. "Don't let those old voices from your teen years make you deaf to the truth."

"You're right. I guess I just need to be reminded that some of the things my foster parents and the other kids used to say don't mean a darn thing."

"They certainly don't. And I'll be happy to remind you whenever I can. So will my *abuelita*, who adores you and wants to know if you'll be able to visit soon. She promised to make green chili and chicken mole, just for you."

Dana laughed. "How can I refuse an offer like that?"

"You can't. So check your calendar and let me know when you can take some time off. And speaking of time, I need to hang up. I'm going to meet the new elementary school principal for coffee."

"Ooh, that sounds interesting."

"He's gorgeous, but who knows? I'll definitely keep you posted."

When the call ended, Dana went for a walk in her neighborhood. She'd no more than returned to the house when her cell phone rang.

It was Sandra Lawson on the line.

"How's Sam doing?" Dana asked.

"He's weak and a little grumpy, but that's probably to be expected after spending more than a week in the hospital. I bought him home about ten minutes ago."

"That's great," Dana said. "I'm so glad to hear that. Is he up to having visitors? I'd love to come by and see you both."

"Yes, of course."

"Don't bother to cook," Dana added. "I'll bring dinner for you when I come. That is, unless someone else has already volunteered."

"No, you and Kieran are the first to know that Sam came home. I was just about to call Pastor Mark next."

"I'm glad I was at the top of your phone list," Dana said. "Give Sam my best and tell him I'll be there around four this afternoon."

As soon as they'd said goodbye and the call ended, Dana pulled out her favorite recipe books so she could start a grocery list. The first one she opened was a 1939 edition of *The Household Searchlight Recipe Book*, which was sure to have some great casseroles. Then she paused midsearch. She'd have to make something heart healthy for Sam, which meant she'd have to do some online research.

Several hours later, after preparing most of the meal, she arrived at the Leaning L. She'd placed the food in containers and packed them in a big cardboard box, which now rested on the front passenger seat. She'd also brought salad fixings, plus a variety of fruit for dessert, all of which she would assemble when she had the use of Sandra's kitchen.

As she steered her car into the yard, she spotted a familiar black Mercedes. Her heart did a series of somersaults that would make a gymnast proud. That is, until reality struck.

Kieran being here wasn't a surprise. Sandra had called him first. She and Sam had missed Rosie terribly and had to be eager to see her.

Dana parked and shut off the ignition, but she continued to sit behind the wheel a moment longer, gathering her thoughts and waiting for her pulse to return to a steady rate. Things had been so awkward when she'd left Kieran's house the other night that she wasn't quite sure what to expect now.

Maybe, since a few days had passed, they'd be able to forget about it and move on. She glanced at her reflection in the rearview mirror. After she'd showered and shampooed her hair, she'd blown it dry, then pulled it into a twist atop her head, using a big, brass clip to hold it in place.

It looked perfectly fine, but Kieran's comment came to mind. *You wore your hair down that evening. It hung nearly to your waist and was so sleek and shiny. The color was even more striking.*

For some silly reason, she reached behind her head, removed the clip and let the strands fall loose. Then, using her fingers, she combed through them.

As she studied her new reflection in the mirror, she was tempted to pull her locks back and clip them up again, just as she did before going into work each day. But she wasn't at the history center now. She was visiting friends, an older couple who treated her like family and a handsome man. What would it hurt to go into the house looking her best?

She blew off her self-doubt, climbed out of the car and circled around to the passenger side to get the cardboard box of food.

As she headed for the house, she berated herself— first for changing her hairstyle and then for stressing about her reason for doing it. The truth was, she found Kieran way too attractive for her own good, and she wasn't going to allow her imagination to run away with her.

Who cared what she looked like? She wouldn't give it another thought. Instead, she continued forward, putting one foot in front of the other and willing her heart to match the slower pace.

Once she'd climbed the steps and crossed the porch, she rang the bell. Moments later, Kieran answered the door.

"Hey," he said, as if he'd had no idea she was coming.

Her heart rate, which hadn't quite righted itself, stumbled for a moment. That is, until a small, happy voice cried out, "Dannnnna!"

At that sweet greeting, warmth filled Dana's chest, and the beats returned to normal. She smiled at the little girl, who wore two neat little pigtails, pale blue bows adorning each one. "Hi, sweetie. It's good to see you."

"Here," Kieran said, taking the cardboard box before Dana could decline. "Let me help you with that."

Releasing her burden was a good thing because, once her hands were free, Rosie practically jumped into her arms.

Dana held the little girl close, relishing the soft scent of baby shampoo and assuming her grandma had fixed her hair today.

Was there anything sweeter and more fulfilling than the love of a child?

"Did you come to see my grandpa?" Rosie asked Dana. "He told me he's all better because I came to see him. And you know what? He's going to get me a pony for my birthday." She held up a hand, her thumb bent to the palm, and showed off her fingers. "I'm gonna be four. And Grandpa said that's big enough to learn how to ride."

"That's awesome," Dana said, although Sam was far from being completely well. Still, seeing Rosie must have lifted his spirits and was sure to be the best medicine of all.

"Looks like we'll be spending a few weekends out here on the Leaning L," Kieran said.

"That's because I'm gonna live with my uncle at his house," Rosie added. "And we're gonna come to the ranch *all* the time so I can visit Grandma and Grandpa and my pony."

Apparently, the adults had already decided that Rosie's temporary living situation would become permanent.

Rosie tugged at the sleeve of Kieran's shirt. "You know what?"

There was no telling, Dana thought, as a smile crossed her lips. The precocious child always had something cute and original to say.

Kieran reached for one of Rosie's pigtails and gave it a gentle tug. "What's that, peanut?"

"Since I'm gonna live with you from now on, I'm gonna call you Uncle Daddy."

Dana had to hand it to the child. She'd not only come up with yet another clever thought, but also a new moniker for the handsome exec. She didn't dare comment. But she did look at Kieran, wondering what he was going to say to that.

Uncle Daddy?

Kieran had no idea how Rosie had come up with a nickname like that, nor did he know how to respond. Back when Rosie had first learned to talk, Zach had referred to Kieran as her uncle. While it had sounded a little odd to him at first, it had touched him in an unexpected way, and he'd soon gotten used to it.

But this was different. Was Rosie making an emotional segue from uncle to daddy? If so, it was more than a little unsettling, especially since he knew he'd never be able to fill Zach's shoes and feared he'd let her down someday.

Kieran glanced at Dana, hoping she'd help him out of this sticky wicket, but she was studying him just as closely as Rosie was. For that reason, the only thing he could think to say was, "Sure. I like that. Can I call you Princess Rosie?"

The little girl clapped her hands, causing Dana to sway with the unexpected movement. "Yes, you can! But call me Princess Rosabelle the Cowboy Girl."

"That's a long name," he said. "Would it be okay if I call you princess for short?"

Rosie nodded, then asked Dana to put her down. "I gotta tell Grandma and Grandpa so they'll know what to call me."

Once Dana bent to place her on the floor, Rosie

dashed off, leaving Dana and Kieran alone in the living room.

When Dana straightened and their gazes met, Kieran was again thrown back into a swirl of surprise and the rush of attraction he'd felt when he'd first answered the door and spotted her on the porch. He hadn't expected to see her at the ranch today, but what really threw him for a blood-rushing loop was the sight of her pretty red hair, glistening as it hung loose along her back and over her shoulders.

He'd nearly complimented her then and there, but before he could find the words to say, Rosie had interrupted them. Should he mention it now? He was tempted to, but he'd really fouled things up by speaking his mind the other night.

"I told Sandra that I'd bring dinner to them," Dana said. "I didn't realize you and Rosie would be here, although I should have. But it doesn't matter. There's plenty for all of us tonight with leftovers for tomorrow."

He couldn't blame her for maintaining ties with Sam and Sandra. She obviously missed Zach and felt his presence whenever she was here on the Leaning L with his parents. "I'll take the box into the kitchen for you."

"Thanks."

Again, he wanted to tell her that he'd noticed her hair, that he liked it. Had she worn it down because of what he'd told her the other night?

Hell, she hadn't expected him to be here today. Leaving it down was probably just a coincidence. It wasn't like she *never* wore it that way.

Shaking off the crazy speculation, he carried the box into the kitchen and placed it on the oak table. Dana, who'd followed him, removed a brown sack, a plastic container and two glass baking dishes.

"What's on the menu?" he asked.

"Baked skinless chicken breasts, brown rice with almonds, a garden salad and a fresh fruit cup for dessert."

Seriously? That sounded rather bland and dull. He'd almost prefer to eat Cowboy Fred's pizza, although he knew better than to say that. "It sounds…"

"Healthy?" She laughed, the lilt of her voice striking a chord deep inside, the vibrations threatening to shatter anything within its range. "Why do I get the feeling that tonight's meal doesn't sound all that tasty to you?"

He chuckled. "Because it…*doesn't*?"

"I wanted to make something that Sam's cardiologist would approve of, and so I did some research. Believe it or not, I'm actually a good cook, even when I'm cutting back on salt, sugar and fat."

"I've never been all that health conscious. But I won't complain."

"Oh, good! Now I won't have to punch you in the eye, like Rosie did to Michael when he annoyed her at Cowboy Fred's."

As much as Kieran wanted to cling tightly to the uneasiness he'd felt after being with Dana the other night, a smile tugged at his lips. "Just so you know, unlike Dragon Boy, I'm actually drawn to ladies in line for the throne."

In fact, he was growing a little too fond of this particular princess, who reminded him of Rapunzel. A man could get lost in hair like hers.

"So how's it going?" Dana asked. "Rosie seems happy, and you don't appear to be nearly as stressed as you did earlier in the week."

"It's getting easier, especially when I'm back at the Leaning L and know that Sandra can take over in a pinch." Actually, now that Dana was here, he felt even better. "So tonight's going to be a piece of cake— even if there isn't a gooey, sweet dessert in sight."

Dana laughed again. "Next time we have dinner together, I'll have to make something gooey and sweet and loaded with carbs and calories just for you."

So there was going to be a next time for them. That was good to know. Apparently, they'd both been able to put Awkward Tuesday behind them.

He supposed he could excuse himself now, but he found it pleasantly entertaining to watch her move about, washing fruits and vegetables, then removing a cutting board and a paring knife from one of the drawers. Obviously, she knew her way around Sandra's kitchen.

"I assume you're also getting used to working from home," she said.

"Not really. I hadn't wanted to hire someone to help me take care of Rosie, but I have a feeling I won't be getting a darn thing done on Tuesdays and Thursdays, so I might be forced to."

Dana began peeling two peaches as well as an

orange and an apple. "Finding a good nanny should solve that problem."

"I'm sure you're right. But for the record, I believe it's a parent's—or in my case, a guardian's—responsibility to raise their kids." He didn't go into detail about the nannies and au pairs he'd had while growing up. Nor did he mention that he'd often felt neglected by his parents.

He'd probably sound like a whiner to a woman who'd been orphaned and raised in foster care.

"I'm probably going to have to bite the bullet," he admitted. "And sooner rather than later. I have to make a business trip to Amarillo on Thursday, although I'll be back in town that same evening. I'm not sure what to do with Rosie while I'm gone. It's not a school day."

"I'd offer to take some vacation time and help you out," Dana said, "but I've got a meeting that day, and I can't reschedule it."

"I was just talking out loud. I wasn't asking for a volunteer." Although, it would have been nice to know Rosie was in Dana's care while he was gone.

Dana reached for the grapes, broke off a small cluster and handed it to Kieran. "Here, have a snack."

He thanked her and popped a couple of red seedless grapes in his mouth.

"I used to live in Amarillo," she said. "And my best friend still works there. Monica Flores. You remember I told you about her?"

He recalled the name. "The librarian, right?"

"Yes. We met at the library near the house where

I lived. She's just graduated from college and landed her first job as a librarian there. She's just a few years older than me, so I found myself talking to her about school, college and scholarships."

"That's great that you've remained friends. Other than Zach, I haven't stayed in contact with any of the other guys who went to school with me."

"Maybe you should look up a few of them."

He shrugged a single shoulder. "Maybe I will— someday. I'm pretty busy at the office, and now that I have Rosie…well, I really don't have any free time."

"I know what you mean. I haven't seen Monica in more than a year, mostly because I moved eight hours away to work at the history center. But we still keep in touch, on the phone and on Facebook." Dana grew pensive. "I really miss having her close."

"I'll be taking the corporate jet to Amarillo," he said, "so you can go with me. That is, if you can get the day off."

She studied him and he got the sneaking feeling he'd stepped over a line. And he probably had. She must think that he was making another move on her when he'd just offered to let her come because he'd wanted to be nice.

"Like I said before," she finally replied, "I've got an appointment. The people I'm meeting have a history foundation and will only be in town Thursday. But thanks for the offer."

"Maybe next time."

Again she studied him, her head tilted slightly to the side, her pretty red hair sluicing down her arm.

"Not that it's any of my business, but what's in Amarillo that can't be done over Skype or FaceTime?"

"Robinson Tech is considering a buyout, and I want to get a tour of their operation."

"That sounds important."

"We've had much bigger deals. I could probably ask someone else to go in my place, but everyone's busy. And I really want to see the outfit for myself. Only trouble is, I don't want to leave Rosie with Sandra while Sam is recovering. And there isn't time to hire a good nanny. Do you know any of the sitters Zach used in the past?"

"There's a teenager who attends Sandra's church. I think her name is Kelly. She's pretty young to have Rosie all day, especially with you so far away. But if you had her watch Rosie at the ranch, Sandra would be here and could oversee things."

"That sounds like a good plan."

"I can probably get time off in the afternoon, after my meeting. So I can come by to help."

It was sweet of her to offer, and he was tempted to take her up on it. Before he could decide, she spoke again.

"You didn't ask. I'm volunteering. Besides, I adore Rosie."

"I know how busy you are, and she isn't your responsibility, but the truth is, I can use all the help and advice I can get."

"I'd be happy to do whatever I can." She tucked a long strand of that gorgeous hair behind her ear. "I promise, if I can't step in or take care of her for whatever reason, I'll let you know. So don't feel bad about calling me if you need me—or if you need anything at all."

Oh, he had needs, all right. But those weren't the ones she was talking about easing. He'd be damned if he'd let her know where his thoughts had strayed, though.

Of course, why wouldn't they? Dana was a beautiful woman, one he was finding more and more attractive every day. Besides, it had been way too long since he'd had sex.

But he wasn't about to let his hormones run away with him.

Chapter Six

Sam might have told Rosie that he was well on the mend thanks to her visit, but he'd been too weak to get out of bed and join the family at the dinner table and remained in his room. When Rosie objected to his eating all by himself, Sandra suggested that she and the little girl have "a picnic" on Grandpa's bed.

That left Dana and Kieran seated alone in the kitchen, a dining experience that felt a little awkward, especially since the handsome man had a way of setting her heart on edge and her sexual awareness on high alert.

And why wouldn't his presence do that to her? All she had to do was take one look at him, with those gorgeous blue eyes and that light brown hair that was always well-groomed, and she was toast. Even now, dressed casually in a pair of designer jeans and a light blue button-down shirt, he commanded a woman's attention. And, he'd certainly captured hers tonight.

"This chicken is really good," he said. "You weren't kidding when you said you know how to cook."

Dana offered him a smile. "I'm glad you like it."

"Who would have guessed that you had a domestic streak?"

"Actually, I don't." For a beat, she wondered if she should be offended by his comment. After all, she had a busy life that wasn't centered at home, even if a man like Kieran wouldn't find it exciting. But after glancing across the scarred oak table and spotting the warmth in his expression and the glimmer in his eyes, she shrugged it off. "Believe it or not, I wasn't interested in cooking until I stumbled across a collection of old cookbooks at an estate sale last year. I began to research how earlier generations ate, so I tried out different recipes. And some of them were pretty tasty."

Kieran sat back in his seat, his grin morphing into a heart-strumming smile. "It sounds like you've picked up a few unique treasures during your shopping escapades."

"I really have. That's what makes shopping for antiques and going to estate sales fun." Again, she glanced at him. Had he found her quirky or odd, like some men did? If he did, his dazzling expression hid it well. "So then, just for the record, I'm not what you'd call a homebody."

"I never thought you were."

Good. But what *had* he thought of her? She certainly didn't frequent the fancy restaurants or attend stellar social events like he and his family and friends did. But then, not many people could afford to. Still, she found her life to be fulfilling. And she was happy with it. So what else mattered?

As they continued to eat, silence stretched between them, interrupted by the occasional sound of a fork clicking on a ceramic plate. Dana tried to focus on finishing her meal, but her hyped-up awareness of the man seated across from her didn't make it easy.

Get a grip, girl. This guy is way out of your league as well as your comfort zone.

And that was so true. Just mention the name *Fortune* and people's interest piqued for a variety of reasons, and not just because of all the charity work done by the Fortune Foundation. Gosh, there was even a royal branch of the family that garnered tabloid headlines!

"Oh," Kieran said, drawing her from her musing. "I nearly forgot. You mentioned a teenager who used to babysit for Zach."

"He called a couple of high school kids occasionally, but the one he used the most was Kelly Vandergrift."

"I'm going to need her phone number. Do you have it? I could ask Sandra, but she'll insist that she can handle watching Rosie for a day. And she really has her hands full with Sam right now."

"You're right." Dana pushed back her chair, the wooden legs scraping the worn, linoleum flooring, and got to her feet. Then she walked to the yellow, wall-mounted telephone and studied the small white-board hanging beside it, where Sandra had written important numbers. She scanned the list until she found Kelly's name. "Here it is. Let me write it down for you so you can take it with you."

Kieran whipped out his cell phone from the clip on his belt. "Just read it off to me. I'll call her now and then add her to my contacts. Even if I hire a full-time nanny, I'm sure I'll need a backup babysitter on occasion."

Moments later, Kelly must have answered, because after Kieran introduced himself and he explained his dilemma. "I realize you might be in school next week, but with Easter coming up, I thought there was a chance you'd be on spring break."

After a slight pause, his face brightened. "Oh, good. I'm glad to hear that. Are you available to watch her on Thursday at the Leaning L?" Again, he listened to Kelly's response, then added, "I'll need you around eight in the morning. Rosie's grandparents will be here, but I don't want them to have to worry about her or to feel as though they need to entertain her."

Kieran laughed. "You, too? In the past week, I've played more games of Candy Land and Go Fish than I can count. Anyway, I really appreciate this, Kelly. I'll have Rosie at the ranch before eight o'clock. I'm not sure how long I'll be gone, but I hope to be back before dark."

After ending the call, Kieran's gaze traveled to Dana. "That worked out great."

"Be sure to give her my phone number," Dana said.

"If she has a problem of any kind while you're in Amarillo, it'll only take me thirty minutes to get here."

"That makes me feel even better, although I hate bothering you, especially when you have a meeting that day, too."

"I really don't mind. I like being helpful."

He studied her a moment. "I didn't know you very well before, but I can now see that you're a special lady. I hadn't expected Zach to fall for a quiet librarian, but I guess there's a lot to be said for that old adage that opposites attract."

Dana wouldn't say that Zach had exactly "fallen" for her. They'd become good friends and gone out whenever he was free or needed a date, but things between them hadn't really clicked. They'd never had the kind of chemistry that made her tingle, or Zach, either, for that matter.

"Actually," she said, "when you get to know me, you'll find that I'm not all that quiet."

As his gaze zeroed in on hers, she tried to gauge his expression, which wasn't at all easy to read. She spotted something warm in his eyes, something soft and…

Darn it. She hoped it wasn't sympathy. She'd gotten so many pitying looks from friends and coworkers who assumed she'd been devastated by Zach's loss.

She'd been saddened, for sure, and disappointed that their relationship had never really gotten off the ground. But her real grief was for the motherless child who was now missing her daddy.

But did she dare admit that to the man who'd been Zach's best friend? She couldn't.

"I should probably know this," Kieran said, "but I never got around to asking Zach. How and when did you two meet?"

"I interviewed him last fall, when I was researching Austin's ranching history. He had a great sense of humor and had me in stitches. A few days later, he called and asked me out to lunch."

Their friendship had evolved into a dating relationship, but that's as far as things went. They'd gone out for six months but there hadn't been anything sexual between them. Something more serious might have developed between them in time, but Rosie's mother, who hadn't stuck around long enough to actually be a mom, had done a real number on his head. So he'd been gun-shy about making a commitment.

They'd talked about it, and while Zach had told Dana she was a "great gal," he said his focus had to be on his daughter. And Dana agreed. When her parents had been alive, they'd been totally committed to her.

Still, instead of pulling away from Zach, she'd been drawn to him, especially to his adorable daughter and his parents, who reminded her of her mom and dad. So her friendship with Zach had worked out nicely for everyone involved.

Then Zach died. Since he'd been her only tie to his family, it was like losing hers all over again.

But she'd never admit anything like that to Kieran. How could she? He'd probably think she was a clingy waif or a family crasher. And she'd walk away from him, Rosie and the Lawsons before she'd ever let that happen.

"I'm sorry for relying on you so much," Kieran said.

"Don't worry about that."

"I'm grateful for all you've done, and it's so easy to turn to you first. But I have a feeling that's making things more difficult for you."

"I'm glad to help. And to be honest, knowing that you, Rosie and the Lawsons need me makes me feel better."

And that was true. The part that complicated matters and made everything worse was her growing attraction to Zach's best friend, especially when Kieran was even more unsuited to her than Zach had been.

When Kieran had left the Leaning L with Rosie the other night, he'd been determined to back off and not rely on Dana too much. She might have said that she wanted to be helpful, but he didn't want to take advantage of her kindness.

Yet even as he came to that conclusion, a small, sarcastic voice piped up, jabbing at him.

How thoughtful—and noble—you are.

He had to admit that there was something else at play, something tempting him to call on her for just about anything. And it wasn't as a friend or as a babysitter who cared about Rosie's well-being. In fact, each time he was with her, he seemed to be more drawn to her, more intrigued by her.

Dana Trevino was a beautiful woman, with a willowy shape, expressive blue eyes and silky red hair a man could run his fingers through. She also had a warm and loving heart, especially with Rosie. And that's what had made her perfect for Zach. Kieran saw that clearly now. She would've been the kind of wife his best friend deserved.

Unlike Kieran, Zach had been both a rancher who loved the land and a man who adored his family. On the other hand, Kieran thrived in the city. And while he might care about his parents and siblings, he'd never been especially close to any of them. At least, he hadn't been in the past. Things were changing now that he'd gotten older and had proven himself to be worthy to step into an executive position at Robinson Tech.

No, it would be better if he left Dana alone so she could lead her own life before he made a complete mess of things. Besides, she still had ties to the Lawsons, and the last thing he wanted to do was to complicate things for the elderly couple who were already dealing with a tragic and painful loss.

Yet even after Kieran and Dana had eaten dinner at the Leaning L the other night and said their goodbyes, thoughts and images of the lovely, kindhearted research librarian continued to drift into his mind.

In fact, even at the office, while he was scheduling the corporate jet for his business trip to Amarillo, he'd thought of her once again and wished she'd been able to join him. And how crazy was that?

No, it was better that he go alone.

When Thursday morning finally rolled around,

Kieran arrived at the Leaning L at a quarter to eight with Rosie in tow, her backpack bulging with dolls, books, sketch pads and markers.

Sandra must have been watching for them, because she met them on the porch before he could knock at the door.

"There's my sweet pea," she said, as she stooped and wrapped Rosie in a warm embrace. "I'm so glad you're here. We're going to have fun today."

Kieran certainly hoped they had an enjoyable—and uneventful—day.

"How's Sam feeling?" he asked.

"A little better. He also seems to be getting stronger." Sandra straightened, then welcomed Kieran with a hug and a kiss on the cheek, an unexpected display of affection that caught him off guard, yet pleased him.

"How about you?" she asked. "Are you holding up all right?"

"Yep. Rosie and I are doing just fine."

"Good," Sandra said, as she led them into the house. "Kelly called a few minutes ago to tell me that she was on her way. That was nice of you to line her up, but you didn't have to. I could have watched Rosie for you."

"I had no doubt about that, but I'll feel better knowing there are two pairs of eyes on her."

And, of course, there was more to it than that. Sam might be responding well to his heart medication and getting stronger each day, but there was no guarantee that he wouldn't have a relapse. And knowing that Kelly would be there to help with Rosie meant Kieran could leave town with a certain confidence.

So once Kelly arrived and Rosie was settled, Kieran drove to the airport and met the company pilot. Then they flew to Amarillo for what he hoped would be a successful business trip.

He returned early that evening, tired and disappointed in the daily operations of the tech company he'd gone to check out.

Now here he was, back at the Leaning L and parked next to Dana's car. Apparently, just as she'd promised, she came by after work to make sure everything was going well while he was gone. He might have planned to back off and not rely on her too much, but he had to admit that he was glad she was here.

Apparently she hadn't felt the same way about cutting ties with him, which pleased him, too.

As he crossed the yard, heading for the house, the screen door swung open, and Dana stepped onto the porch. She wore a pair of black slacks and a white blouse, typical business attire and an attractive look. But what struck him was her hairstyle, which was pulled up into a soft, feminine style topknot like something a woman in the late 1800s might wear. He had no idea what to call it, but the term *Gibson Girl* came to mind.

He nearly complimented her, but the words jammed in his throat. How did a man go about telling a woman like Dana that she was beautiful and unpredictable without making her think he was interested in her?

Especially if he didn't want her or anyone else to suspect that he was.

Damn. Here he was, approaching Zach's house with an idea that was so inappropriate it was hard for him to admit, even to himself.

"How did things go today?" he asked her.

Dana lifted her index finger to her lips as if making a shushing sound. When he reached the porch and was within hearing distance, she lowered her voice to a whisper. "Everything went well, but Rosie's asleep."

Kieran glanced at his watch. "Isn't it a little late for a nap? Or is it early for bed?"

"She and Kelly had a big day, so she had a hard time winding down. She finally crashed about thirty minutes ago."

"It sounds like she had fun. But how did Sam and Sandra do?"

"They were delighted to have her, but Sam said he was tuckered out, too. I think he's asleep now. And Sandra is sitting in the living room with her feet up."

"In that case, I don't want to interrupt her quiet time." Kieran probably ought to take a seat on the porch and wind down from his own busy day, but he found himself asking Dana, "Are you up for a walk?"

"Sure." She carefully shut the screen door, then followed him down the steps and into the yard. "So how did your meeting in Amarillo go?"

"Not as well as I'd hoped. I wasn't impressed with the operation or their financials. So once I got back on the jet, I emailed the board of directors and advised against that buyout."

Then I'd say the trip went well. Your time wasn't wasted if you saved the company from making a bad investment."

"That's true." He glanced at the setting sun, which had streaked the western horizon in shades of pink, orange and gray.

"I hope you don't mind," Dana said, "but once I got here, I told Kelly she could go home. I also paid her."

"That's fine. Just let me know how much I owe you."

"Forty dollars," she said.

For some reason, he felt more indebted to Dana than that, which was a little disconcerting, although he wasn't sure why. When he'd mentioned that he hadn't wanted to make things difficult for her by asking too much of her, she'd insisted that helping him with Rosie made her feel better.

Why was that? The only answer he came up with was that being with Rosie, especially on the Leaning L, provided her with a connection to Zach. If that was the case, and Kieran suspected that it was, it just proved that she was clinging to his memory.

He stole a glance her way. She was studying the western horizon and what was turning out to be an amazing sunset. Yet it was Dana's beauty and the pretty copper color of her hair that struck him as gaze-worthy.

If things were different, if she'd never dated Zach, Kieran might suggest they take a bottle of wine and the Lawsons' all-terrain vehicle out to a quiet spot by the pond, where they could watch a waning sunset turn into a cozy, romantic evening.

As tempting as the thought might be, it was a bad idea. The last thing in the world he needed to do was make a move on Dana, who might never forget Zach.

Kieran had fought long and hard to stand out in his family and at Robinson Tech, and he'd succeeded. So he wasn't about to take a back seat to anyone, even if that guy had once been the best friend he'd ever had.

As Dana and Kieran passed a corral on their aimless walk to nowhere in particular, she didn't want it to end. The light breeze refreshed her after a day's work indoors, and so did the sights and sounds of the ranch preparing for nightfall. But it was the man beside her that commanded her full attention.

His swagger and his musky scent stirred a longing deep in her soul. When her shoulder inadvertently bumped his arm, his male presence slammed into her, creating thoughts that were way too romantic for her own good. And for one long beat, her heart stalled.

The weathervane creaked and a horse whinnied in the distance. Yet her thoughts centered on the man beside her who was so close that she could have easily reached out and taken his hand in hers, a move that seemed like the most natural thing in the world for her to do. But she'd never been that bold.

Instead she relied on her vivid imagination, which allowed her to live vicariously through the novels she read or the many historical figures who often came alive after she'd researched them at the center.

But Kieran Fortune was made of flesh and blood, a millennial man who wasn't the kind of hero a woman like her should even dream about. If she were to act on her silly romantic musings, she'd regret it for the rest of her life.

That might sound as if she thought she was unworthy of him, which wasn't true. She had a solid self-image. She just preferred not to hobnob with the rich and famous. And that's what he was.

People wrote magazine and newspaper articles about men like him all the time, which reminded her of the phone call she received earlier today.

"There's something I thought I'd better tell you," she said. "A journalist contacted me at the history center today and asked if she could set up an appointment to meet with me and to do some research for an article she's writing."

Kieran continued the pace they'd set, but he glanced at Dana with a quizzical expression. "And...?"

Apparently, he wasn't sure why she'd brought up something that was practically an everyday occurrence where she worked, but there was a good reason she wanted him to know.

"Her name is Ariana Lamonte, and she's profiling the 'new Fortunes' for her blog. Then she's going to merge the stories into an article for *Weird Life* magazine."

At that, Kieran's steps slowed to a near standstill. "I've heard about her. She interviewed my sister Sophie and my half brother, Keaton Whitfield."

Dana wasn't sure how to respond, since Kieran

probably had no idea how much she knew about his family. It wasn't all that much, but Zach had told her that several of Kieran's half siblings had turned up recently. Apparently, Gerald Robinson aka Jerome Fortune had been a real Romeo, although Zach had used the word *horndog* in relating the story.

"Ariana mentioned her interest in old newspapers and magazines," Dana said. "I can't deny her access to the archives, but under the circumstances, I thought you should know what she's planning to write."

Kieran took a deep breath, then slowly let it out. "It's no big secret that my dad cheated on my mom. Not just once, but time and again. And with our involvement in the Fortune Foundation as well as Peter's Place, a lot of people are probably curious about us."

They might wonder why, when Gerald Robinson had never admitted to having once been known as Jerome Fortune, although Kieran and his siblings had each added on the Fortune name. They also might want to know why he'd staged his own death when he left his family ties behind—another detail Zach had revealed—and why he'd changed his name before creating a billion-dollar tech company.

Dana might have asked Kieran for details since she counted herself as one of many people intrigued by the Fortune Robinson clan—particularly Kieran—but she kept her thoughts to herself. She'd simply have to be satisfied with what Zach had revealed and what little Kieran imparted.

"Besides," Kieran added, "Ms. Lamonte's article

might be good publicity for Robinson Tech as well as the Fortune Foundation."

"You're probably right. I'm glad you're not worried about it."

He shrugged. "I'm not proud of the things my father did, although I do admire his brilliance and his business acumen."

"Zach admired that, too."

Kieran merely nodded. "But I appreciate the heads-up, Dana. So thanks for letting me know, even though there isn't much I can do about stories like that getting out."

She smiled. "That's what friends are for."

But when their gazes locked, something more than a friendly look passed between them. Before she could convince herself that she might be reading him wrong, he lifted his hand and cupped her jaw. "You're amazing."

Her cheeks warmed, and when his thumb stroked her skin, she tingled from head to toe. For a moment, she thought he might kiss her.

But he didn't. In fact, he didn't move at all, and neither did she. Heck, she was afraid to even breathe for fear he'd remove his hand before she'd had a chance to savor his touch.

Should she ask him what his words and his gesture meant? Maybe, but her heart was fluttering so hard she thought it might fly away, and the words jammed in her throat. Unfortunately, about the time she nearly got her act together, his hand slid off her face. Then he tore his gaze away.

When he continued to walk, she fell into step beside him again. He didn't say another word as they circled the barn and headed back to the house. She wasn't ready to end the short time they'd spent together, and an ache settled deep in her chest.

She was, however, eager to read Ariana Lamonte's article when it came out. She was especially interested in the Fortune family now. And she found Kieran more intriguing than ever. So much so, that she'd be tempted to dip her toe into his world and try it on for size.

How was that for having a vivid imagination and creating a pipe dream that would never come true?

Chapter Seven

Kieran couldn't believe how close he'd come to kissing Dana last night. But when he'd gazed into her blue eyes, he'd nearly met a sweet death. His brains deserted him, and he'd reached out and touched her face.

That was bad enough, but then he'd brushed his thumb across her cheek, felt the softness of her skin, and his hormones had shot into overdrive. For a moment, he'd forgotten who she was.

And that was a big mistake. Thankfully, he'd finally wrapped his mind around what he'd almost done, and he'd come to a screeching halt and walked away. But the damage had already been done, and he had no idea how to correct it.

Dana must have been uncomfortable, too, because once they got back to the house, she'd quickly said her goodbyes, mentioning something about a neighbor who needed her to do a favor. But he'd wager that had only been an excuse to escape him—and one that was only slightly better than having to shampoo her hair.

Needless to say, he couldn't call her anymore to ask for her help. He couldn't risk the temptation. Because next time, he just might take her in his arms and kiss her senseless. And then he'd be in a real fix.

He needed to get contact numbers for other babysitters for when he was at the office and in meetings, but he couldn't ask Sandra. She'd insist upon watching Rosie herself, and she already had too much on her plate. Besides, her health wasn't the best.

Still, that meant he had to come up with something else—or rather, some*one* else. Someone permanent to look after Rosie for him.

For that reason, on Friday morning he'd spent an hour on the phone with an agency that provided experienced nannies for working families. Then he spent most of Saturday interviewing several potential caregivers.

He settled on Megan Baker, a reasonably attractive brunette in her late twenties, and asked her to show up bright and early on Tuesday morning. He would be going into the office, no longer working from home now that he'd hired a nanny who would solve his problem once and for all.

Megan was friendly and outgoing. She also seemed competent, so he'd left Rosie in her care. But after he returned from work Tuesday afternoon and Megan had left, Rosie met him in the kitchen with her arms crossed, her little face scrunched into a frown.

"What's wrong, princess?"

"I don't like her."

The new nanny had seemed nice enough to him. "You mean Megan? Why not?"

Rosie harrumphed, then unfolded her arms and slapped her hands on her hips. "Because she ate the pink ice cream *all gone*. And she made me eat the chocolate, even when I don't like it. Then she filled up her bowl again and wouldn't even share it with me. And she only wanted to watch TV. And even when I said please, she wouldn't play or color or read stories with me."

At that, Kieran decided he didn't like Megan, either.

"I'll tell you what, Rosie. We'll find a different nanny—one who *will* play with you and share the strawberry ice cream."

She made her way to where he stood, then lifted her arms to him, indicating she wanted him to pick her up. When he did, she rested her head against his and asked, "Why can't I just stay with you, Uncle Daddy? I'll be really, really good."

His heart swelled with myriad emotions, only one of which was remorse at having to leave her with a sitter. "Because I have to go into the office. And I also have to attend a lot of boring meetings."

In spite of the guilt, a flutter of pride rose in his chest. It was nice to know that she preferred to be with him.

So the next morning, after taking her to preschool, he told the agency that he wouldn't need Megan anymore and moved on to the next nanny candidate.

Darla Sue Williams, a maternal, heavyset woman in her midfifties, seemed to be the perfect choice. So when she arrived bright and early on Thursday morning, he again headed for the office. But when he returned just after five that evening, and after Darla Sue had waddled out the door, he turned to Rosie, who stood before him, frowning yet again.

But this time, he knew what was wrong. The little princess had found fault with nanny number two.

"I take it you didn't like Darla Sue, either," he said.

Rosie crossed her arms and shifted her weight to one hip. "She can't sit down on the floor and color with me 'cause she broke her knee one day and has Arthur Right Us in it. And when she was still eating lunch and I was going to play with my dolls, she let out a big toot and didn't say 'scuse me."

"She probably thought that you hadn't heard her."

Rosie rolled her eyes and sighed. "Then she has broken ears, too, because it was really loud and I think everyone in the world heard it."

Kieran bit back a laugh. There was no pleasing this kid, although he had to admit Darla Sue might not be the perfect fit, either. But now what?

"Uncle Daddy," Rosie said, "can't you work right here like you did before? I just want to be with *you*."

Damn. The blond-haired princess was too adorable for words, and it warmed his heart to know that she'd rather be with him—even if that wasn't possible.

The most obvious solution was to increase the number of days she spent at preschool, but he'd tried doing that the first week she'd moved in with him. Miss Peggy, the preschool director, said she was sorry, but they were full. She then offered to add Rosie to the waiting list, which had seemed fair enough. That is, until Kieran learned there were already more than a dozen names on it.

"I'm sure that's not what you wanted to hear," Miss Peggy had said. When he agreed, she'd added, "You may not know this, but we have one of the best preschools in Austin."

"Super," he'd said, although he'd wondered if it might help Rosie's chances of moving up to the top of the list if he made a donation of some kind. But the school wasn't a nonprofit organization. Besides, a move like that smacked of something his father might try to pull.

So that left only one thing for Kieran to do. He'd have to take Rosie to the office with him next Tuesday morning, because there was no way he'd call Dana— no matter how badly he wanted to.

At five minutes to one o'clock on Wednesday, right after Dana returned to work from lunch, a twenty-something brunette arrived at the history center.

Normally Dana didn't assess the visitors, but this one was attractive and had an interesting Bohemian style. Dressed in high-heeled boots, flared jeans and a paisley tunic top, the woman also carried a floppy, soft leather purse, a loose leaf notebook and a padded laptop case.

"I'm Ariana Lamonte," she said. "I spoke to someone on the telephone last week and made an appointment to do some research today."

"Actually, you talked to me." Dana reached out and shook Ariana's hand. "You're doing an article on the new Fortunes for your blog and for *Weird Life* magazine."

"That's right." Ariana smiled, as she wrapped Dana's hand in a strong, confident grip. "I came to check the archives for newspapers and magazines from about thirty years ago."

"No problem. But before I take you to the reading room, you'll need to sign in at the front desk."

Ariana did as instructed.

"You'll also have to place your bags in one of our lockers," Dana added.

At that, Ariana shot her a questioning look.

"We ask everyone to do that so we can ensure the security and preservation of our material."

"I understand," Ariana said. "But what about my laptop? I'd like to take notes, if that's all right."

"As long as you lock up the case, you can have the laptop."

"What about my cell phone?"

"If you take it out of your purse, you can have that, too."

"Perfect. Are there any other rules I should be aware of?"

"They're posted on the wall," Dana said. "But if

you want to take any handwritten notes, you can't use a pen. I can provide a pencil and notepaper. And once you're in the reading room, if you'd like a specific magazine or newspaper, you'll have to fill out a call slip. One of the staff will get it for you."

"I understand. And I guess it's safe to assume that I can't check out anything, and that all the material needs to stay on the premises."

"That's right."

After Ariana signed in, Dana took her first to the lockers. After she put away her bags, she took her to the reading room.

"Let me know if I can get anything for you," Dana said.

"Thank you." Ariana smiled. "I'll do that."

About an hour later, after requesting several different magazines and studying various microforms for news articles, Ariana began to close up her laptop.

"Did you find everything you were looking for?" Dana asked.

"Not really."

"What were you looking for?" Dana asked.

"At least a hint of why Jerome Fortune went to such extremes when he left home and changed his name to Gerald Robinson."

Dana wasn't about to say it, but from what she'd heard, Gerald's children all seemed to have accepted whatever reason he might have had. So who was she to question them?

"But that doesn't mean my research was a bust," Ariana said. "One of the interviews I read implied that Gerald Robinson came to Austin nursing a broken heart, and that Charlotte Prendergast helped him pick up the pieces."

That must be true. The couple had married and gone on to have eight children, one of whom was Kieran.

Dana had gotten most of her information from Zach, who hadn't told her a lot. But she knew that Gerald, or rather Jerome, had lost his father and had been rejected by his mother. Zach hadn't gone into detail, but she'd assumed that things had gotten so unbearable that Jerome Fortune had staged his own death, then changed his name.

"There's a lot to sort through," Ariana said.

"He was probably grief stricken by his father's death and hurt by his mother's rejection." Dana had no more than uttered the assumption out loud when she wished she could reel it back in. After all, she wasn't a family member and didn't know the facts.

"Maybe," Ariana said, "but I have reason to believe there was more to it than that."

Dana wasn't sure what the journalist meant, although she was curious and tempted to prod for more details. But she didn't want Ariana to think she had a personal interest in that article. And she really didn't.

She wasn't a Fortune and never would be.

Kieran's decision to take Rosie to the office with him the following Tuesday morning had seemed like a good idea at the time, but it hadn't worked out that way.

Sure, everyone at Robinson Tech had oohed and

aahed over the precocious little girl, who'd sat at the receptionist's desk for an hour that morning and chatted with each employee and guest. Then Karen, his administrative assistant, had taken her into the break room and given her something to drink and a granola bar for a snack. Things went well until Rosie dropped a full, adult-size glass of OJ, scattering broken glass and sticky juice all over the floor.

For lunch, Kieran took her to Gregorio's, a trendy Italian deli, for lunch. He ordered macaroni and cheese for her, but she pushed it aside after taking a single bite.

"What's the matter?" he asked.

"It's not the right kind. I like the mac and cheese that comes out of the box. This kind is yucky."

Kieran would have preferred Gregorio's variety, especially since they made the pasta on the premises and used three different types of cheese for the sauce. But what was he supposed to do if she wouldn't eat?

As a result, he ordered the chicken tenders to go.

By two o'clock, he realized she needed a nap. So he removed the cushions from the two chairs in front of his desk and made a small bed for her on the floor. She might have dozed off, but his phone rang several times, causing her to stir.

An hour later, he gave up and let her sit at his desk to color. But she must have left the cap off the orange marker for days, if not longer, because it was dry as a bone. Apparently, that was the only color she could possibly use to draw a butterfly, so she had a meltdown.

At that point, he gave up and took her home.

He hadn't thought that being a parent would be easy, but he hadn't had any idea how tough the job really was. Nor had he realized it would make it damn near impossible to get any work done.

And that wasn't the only thing that had suffered since he brought Rosie to live with him. His love life was at a complete standstill.

If he'd had a relationship with someone right now, he might actually have a love life. And that realization made him wonder why he'd been such a commitment phobe in the first place.

Not that he was sorry he had Rosie. He actually enjoyed being with her—when he didn't have any work or projects that needed to get done.

On Wednesday morning, while at the preschool, he asked the director if Rosie had moved up on the wait-list to attend full time. She had, but only by one child. "I'm not sure how helpful this will be," Miss Peggy added. "One of our families is on vacation this week, so we can let Rosie take her place this Thursday."

Kieran had thanked her, relieved that he had child care for the rest of the week. But then he received word on Friday afternoon that the board of directors had scheduled an important meeting on Saturday morning.

He'd called Kelly as soon as he'd heard the news, but she was on a camping trip with a friend's family. Even the nanny agency couldn't help since the office was closed for the weekend. So it was official: he'd run out of child care options once again.

That is, until Dana crossed his mind. Once he envisioned her smiling face, her long, silky hair, those expressive blue eyes...well, hope soared.

In spite of his resolve to avoid her, he had no other choice than to call her. And with each ring of the phone, his mood lightened even more.

For a moment, he worried that she might not answer, then he heard her sweet voice dance across the line. "Hi, Kieran. What's up?"

"I'm having nanny problems," he blurted out. Realizing his desperation had run away with him, he added, "I'm not asking you to help with that, but do you know of any other people Zach might have used to watch Rosie when Kelly wasn't available? I'm talking about adult women Rosie might actually like."

"He had a few girls he'd call sometimes, but they're all teenagers and not available as full-time sitters. I'm afraid Sandra was always his first choice."

And Sandra wasn't going to be an option these days.

Kieran raked a hand through his hair and blew out a sigh of frustration. "I have a meeting tomorrow that I can't miss or reschedule. And I really dread the thought of taking Rosie with me." Did he dare tell her he knew firsthand why that wasn't going to work?

"I can watch her for you," Dana said.

In spite of his resolve, relief washed over him. Dana had come to his rescue yet again.

"But if you don't mind," she added, "I'd rather you brought her to my house. That way, we can play dress up."

"What's that?" Kieran asked, although he suspected Rosie wouldn't object to anything Dana suggested.

"It's just something we do—a game, actually."

Then Rosie would definitely be on board for that. "You have no idea how much I appreciate that offer."

Nor did she realize how much he was looking forward to seeing her again.

On Saturday morning, Kieran drove to Dana's place in Hyde Park. Dana had told him that she'd renovated one of the homes that had been built right after World War II. But nothing prepared him for what he saw when he pulled up in front of the small, wood-framed house that was painted mustard yellow. The roof and shutters were dark brown, while the porch and window were framed in white, the front door a bright orange.

He doubted it was much bigger than 1200 square feet, but the exterior seemed to suit Dana. And so did the well-manicured yard, with freshly mowed grass and a variety of orange and yellow marigolds lining the walkway.

In fact, he sat in the car a moment, just studying the unique decor and style. He had no idea what the place had looked like when she purchased it, but she'd done an amazing job with the renovation. No wonder she wanted to keep the house for a while before selling it. She ought to enjoy the fruits of her labor.

"Can I get out of my car seat?" Rosie asked. "I can do it myself."

"Sure, princess." Kieran slid out from behind the

wheel, circled the car and opened the rear passenger door for the little girl who was determined to unbuckle herself.

"See?" Rosie said, clearly proud of her efforts. Then she reached for her backpack and hurried up the walkway to the front porch.

Dana, his beautiful lifesaver, opened the door and greeted them with a bright-eyed smile before Rosie could ring the bell.

The child practically jumped with glee, and Kieran's heart reacted the same way. Damn, he hadn't realized how badly he'd missed her.

"Just wait until you see what I have planned for us to do this morning," Dana told the happy little girl.

"Can we go to the park again?" Rosie asked. "Like we did last time I came here?"

"If you want to. But first, we're going to make old-fashioned sugar cookies with sprinkles. Then we're going to play dress up."

Rosie glanced over her shoulder at Kieran, a smile stretched across her face. "You don't have to come back and pick me up until nighttime, Uncle Daddy."

Now, that was the kind of reaction every parent hoped their child would have when dropping them off at day care or with a sitter.

Kieran looked over the child's head at Dana and winked. "Don't worry. I'll be back sooner than that."

"It really doesn't matter to me. We have a full day planned, especially if we pack a lunch and go to the park." Dana placed a gentle hand on Rosie's head, taking a moment to stroke her hair. "Honey, why don't you take your things into the living room?"

Rosie slipped past Dana and hurried into the house, taking her backpack with her. That left the adults alone on the porch, which wasn't nearly as awkward as he'd once thought it would be.

"Before you go," Dana said, "I want to share something with you. A couple of days ago, when Ariana Lamonte came by the history center and researched some old magazines and newspaper articles, I assumed she was interested in your father's move to Austin and the formation of Robinson Tech."

That's what Kieran had thought, too. "What was she looking for?"

"I'm not entirely sure. Apparently, she uncovered an article that suggested your father came to town brokenhearted, and that your mother helped put him on the mend."

"I can see how my mom would have helped him forget the life he once had as Jerome Fortune."

"Maybe, but when I implied something similar, Ariana said she wasn't so sure and suggested there was more to it than that."

Kieran bristled at the thought of a journalist digging into his father's past. Sure, his old man had kept a lot of secrets from the family for years. But what appeared to be an article about the younger Fortunes was sounding more like an exposé of Gerald Robinson aka Jerome Fortune.

Recently, thanks to their dad's numerous affairs, they'd met several half siblings they hadn't realized existed. Kieran had been a little embarrassed by it, but that didn't mean he wasn't curious about the past.

He couldn't very well blame Ariana for her interest in the family, but the fact that there might be some old skeletons for her to uncover didn't sit well with him.

At first when he'd heard about the article she was writing, he'd thought highlighting some of the younger Fortunes might be good publicity for the company as well as for the Fortune Foundation and Peter's Place, a home for wayward teenage boys his brother Graham had established. But now he feared it might have the opposite effect.

He wouldn't mention that to Dana, though. Instead, he shrugged it off, pretending it didn't interest him in the least.

"Nothing about my father would surprise me," he said, glancing at his wristwatch.

"You'd better go," Dana said.

"You're right. I still have to drive across town, and I don't want to be late for that meeting."

Dana glanced over her shoulder and into the living room, where Rosie was already unloading her books and markers. "And don't worry about us. We're going to have fun today."

Kieran didn't doubt that. He took a moment to study the pretty redhead who had proven to be a good friend. "I know I've told you this before, but it's true. I really appreciate you."

And not just for helping him out as a sitter.

Dana's smile set off a glimmer in her eyes. "And like I said, I'm happy to do it."

The morning sun cast a shimmer of gold in her auburn hair. Framed within the doorway of her newly painted house, the colors reminding him of fall, she seemed to fit nicely, leaving her mark on the decor in a special way.

"I love what you've done to this house." And he did, which was odd coming from a man who made it a point to never use the *L* word, especially when he was with a single woman who might get the wrong idea about him.

But this woman was different, and whenever he was around her, he felt a lot of different emotions stirring up inside him.

"Thanks," she said. "When you come back for Rosie, I'll give you a tour of the inside."

"I'd lo…like that." Then he did something completely unexpected—he leaned forward, cupped her jaw and brushed a kiss on her cheek.

A show of affection like that wouldn't have been so bad. But when he caught a whiff of her scent… Was that Coco Chanel? If not, it was a darn good knockoff. It also knocked him off stride. And rather than end the thanks-and-goodbye kiss, his lips lingered on her cheek a beat too long.

Dammit. What was wrong with him?

He needed this woman in the worst way. Maybe even in the *best* way. And he was really going to screw things up if he wasn't careful.

"I'm sorry if I just stepped over the line or dishonored Zach in any way."

"You didn't," she said, her eyes wide, her lips parted.

If she knew what he was thinking, she'd disagree.

"I'll be back in a couple of hours," he said.

"Take all the time you need."

He nodded, then turned to go, knowing that he was going to need a hell of a lot more time to get his racing pulse under control and his mind back on track.

Chapter Eight

Dana stood on the front porch and watched Kieran head to his car, the skin on her cheek still tingling from the soft touch of his lips and the warmth of his breath.

If he'd meant that kiss to be a friendly show of appreciation, then why had he apologized for it? That hadn't made sense, unless he'd had another reason behind it.

She could probably ponder the possibilities until the cows came home, but that'd be a waste of time. She didn't have a lot of experience with men or in reading their intentions, especially wealthy corporate executives. So she wouldn't continue to stand on her stoop, stunned by their latest awkward encounter.

As she turned around so she could go back into

her house, she stole one last peek at Kieran, who was getting into his car.

He glanced over his shoulder at the same time, catching her in the act of gawking at him like a love-struck wallflower at a high school dance.

Unsure of what—if anything—she should do, she lifted her hand and gave him a casual wave, as if she hadn't been affected by either the kiss or the eye contact. Then she passed through the doorway and into the living room, where Rosie was seated on the hardwood floor, coloring.

It had been a month or more since Rosie had last been at Dana's house. That day had started with a trip to the library for the preschool story hour. Then they'd picked up sandwiches at a nearby deli and spent the next couple hours at the park. When they returned home, Dana pulled out some of her vintage clothing and let Rosie dress up like a "big lady," including an application of pink lipstick.

Rosie probably expected more of the same today, but Dana had a better idea, one that was going to be both fun and educational.

As she approached the little girl, Dana said, "I have a surprise for you."

Rosie looked up, her eyes bright, and smiled. "What is it?"

"The other day, when I was shopping at an estate sale, I found an antique chest called a steamer trunk. I bought it so that I could refurbish it. But when I got it home and opened it, I found a treasure inside."

Rosie's eyes grew wide. "Like gold?"

"No, not that kind. A treasure can also mean something special to the person who finds it." When Rosie scrunched her face and tilted her head, Dana reached out her hand and wiggled her fingers. "Come with me."

Rosie pushed aside her coloring book, got to her feet and took Dana's hand. "Where is it?"

"In my guest room. I'll show it to you."

Moments later, as they stood in front of the hundred-year-old trunk that appeared well-traveled, Dana lifted the lid, revealing the old clothing and stage props inside.

A playbill, its pages yellowed and worn, suggested she'd found costumes that had been made for the cast of a 1936 theater performance about Texas pioneers. Along with a few bonnets, skirts, blouses, a man's britches and a red flannel shirt, there was also a child-size calico dress.

At the time she'd discovered the treasure trove, Dana had immediately thought about Rosie. But before she could invite her over for a playdate, she'd gotten the call about Zach's accident, so the plan had never panned out.

Now, with Rosie here, today seemed to be the perfect time to play dress up while having a history lesson and making homemade cookies.

"Instead of going to the library," Dana said, as she began removing a woman's long, blue skirt and the child's calico dress, "let's put on these costumes and have story hour here."

"Those clothes look funny," Rosie said.

"Maybe to those of us living today, but a hundred and fifty years ago, people dressed like this."

"Okay. That'll be fun." Rosie kicked off her pink sneakers and began removing her white T-shirt and denim shorts.

"After we get dressed like pioneers, I'll tell you real life stories about people who lived in Texas a long time ago. And then we'll whip up a batch of sugar cookies from a recipe I found in an old cookbook."

"Will we make enough cookies so Uncle Daddy can have one, too?"

"We certainly will. And we'll also have plenty for you to take home."

Then, when Kieran returned for Rosie...

Dana's thoughts stalled on the handsome man who'd kissed her, then quickly apologized and dashed off to a business meeting. Her cheek was no longer tingling. But that didn't change the fact that Kieran Fortune had kissed her, that his lips and his soft breath had warmed her from the inside out. The affection he'd shown her had touched her in a magical way, transporting her into an unexpected role, like an actress on the stage.

Dana might try to forget what had happened when he left, but that brief kiss and the romantic fantasy it provoked would remain in her memory for a very long time.

The board meeting at the Robinson Tech office had gone into overtime, lasting several more hours than anyone had expected. So by the time Kieran returned for Rosie, it was nearly one o'clock.

After parking at the curb in front of Dana's house, he made his way along the marigold flanked walkway to the front porch. He rang the bell, and moments later, Rosie answered the door wearing a long prairie-style dress, a floppy yellow bonnet and a happy smile.

But what really took him by surprise—and a pleasant one at that—was seeing Dana dressed like a schoolmarm in a long blue skirt and a white, high-collared blouse, her hair swept up in a soft, feminine topknot.

"What's going on?" he asked, unable to quell an erupting chuckle.

"We've been playing pioneer girls." Rosie lifted a small glass jar that held something white and gooey. "And look what we made!"

Kieran didn't have any idea what that stuff was.

When Rosie handed him the jar for a closer inspection, he still didn't have a clue and furrowed his brow.

"It's butter," Dana said.

"Yep." Rosie beamed. "We put milk in this jar, then we put a lid on it."

"Actually, we didn't use milk," Dana corrected. "It was heavy cream."

"Uh-huh," Rosie said, nodding in agreement. "Then I had to shake and shake and shake until my arm got tired. So Dana helped me until it turned into butter. It's not yellow, but it's just like the kind they used to make when my grandma was a little girl and they didn't get to buy it in the store."

"Awesome." Kieran snuck a glance at Dana, who stood before him like a beautiful, red-haired lady from days gone by.

"We not only had a history lesson," Dana said, "but we also had fun while you were gone."

"I can see that." Kieran was growing more and more impressed with Dana's finer qualities each time he saw her.

She gave a little shrug. "I guess there's no secret that I have a quirky side."

"No, you can't hide it from me any longer. But for the record, I think you're the cutest teacher I've ever met."

Her flush deepened, and he glanced away. The last thing he needed to do was to get caught up in his attraction again. But like it or not, he found her adorable, quirks and all.

And there lay the problem. He needed to shake off the romantic musing. So in an effort to do just that, he scanned the inside of her nicely decorated home, which had a retro vibe that suited the house and the neighborhood as well as the owner.

But he didn't just get a visual of her home. The sweet aroma of vanilla filled the living room. "I take it you pioneers also found time to do some baking today."

"We made cookies," Rosie said. "And there's a special one just for you. I put a lot of pink sprinkles on it because that's my favorite color. But you can't eat it until you have lunch. That's what Dana said."

"Sounds fair to me." Kieran gave Dana a wink.

"Can we go to the park now?" Rosie asked. "Dana made sandwiches and apples and stuff. We're going to have a picnic."

Kieran turned to Dana. The invitation to join them should come from her. After all, she'd been entertaining Rosie the entire morning. Maybe she wanted to take a break.

"I made plenty for all of us," she said. "Are you hungry?"

Kieran's brother Ben, the president of Robinson Tech, had brought in breakfast burritos for everyone at the meeting, so he wasn't starving.

"I've never been one to turn down food," he said, "especially if I can share a light meal with two pioneer girls."

Dana blessed him with a pretty smile. "Does that mean you're up for an afternoon at the park?"

In spite of his earlier resolve to avoid Dana, he'd be happy to join in any activity if it included her. "Sure. Why not?"

"Goodie!" Rosie clapped her hands.

When Dana instructed her to go change her clothes, she took off, dashing down the hall, the skirt of her prairie dress sweeping the hardwood floor.

"While she's gone," Dana said, "I have a question for you."

"What's that?"

"Why did you apologize for kissing my cheek when you left this morning?"

Her cheek. Right. It's not as though he'd kissed her on the lips, which he'd been tempted to do.

"That kiss was impulsive, and since I know how much you cared about Zach, I didn't want you to think I was trying to…"

"Take his place?"

"Yeah, I guess that's it." A lot of people might have thought that a computer whiz kid and a cowboy might be unlikely friends, but they'd loved each other like brothers.

"I thought that kiss was sweet. And that it was appreciative of our…friendship."

"I'm glad. I guess I'm the only one stressing about it." Kieran raked a hand through his hair.

She might have just let him off the hook but he was still struggling with what he'd done. He couldn't help thinking that it should be Zach standing in Dana's living room, overwhelmed by his sexual attraction to the pretty redhead. It should be Zach looking forward to taking his sweet daughter to the park for a picnic.

But Zach was gone. And the woman and child he'd left behind were burrowing deep into Kieran's heart. And something about that felt wrong.

"Just for the record," Dana said, "Zach and I weren't as involved as people might think."

Kieran merely nodded. In a way, it was a relief to know they hadn't been talking marriage or engagement. But just because Dana and Zach hadn't been too serious didn't mean they hadn't been sexually involved. And that's what made him so leery about the idea of dating her.

Striking up a romance was sure to lead to more kissing and eventually to making love. And as appealing as that might sound, Kieran didn't feel right about taking his best friend's girl to bed, even if that friend was dead.

Hell, Zach was one of the greatest guys Kieran had ever known—honest, hardworking, dependable and loyal. Yet life had never been especially easy for him, especially financially.

What had he done wrong? Why did he have to die so young, before he'd experienced love and happiness?

On the other hand, Kieran had it all. Not that things had been perfect for him growing up. But unlike Zach, he'd never had to worry about financing his college education, caring for aging parents who weren't in the best of health, trying to turn things around for a struggling ranch or being a single dad.

There seemed to be something wrong about stepping in and taking Zach's place.

And it was too bad Kieran felt that way. Because that was the *only* thing holding him back from admitting his feelings for Dana.

After a short five-minute drive, Dana, Kieran and Rosie pulled up at Westside Park, Austin's newest recreational spot for families.

"I hope I'm not the only kid here," Rosie said.

Dana hoped so, too. Rosie didn't like to play alone, and if there weren't any other children on the playground, she'd want the adults to swing and slide with her. They'd had a lot of fun this morning, but Dana was ready to sit back and enjoy a picnic lunch in the fresh air and sunshine.

"It's Saturday," Kieran said. "I'm sure you'll find plenty of kids to play with."

And he was right. By the time he parked the car, they had a clear view of the grassy play area, with its Western-themed climbing structure and big yellow slide in the shape of a giant sombrero.

"Will you look at that?" Kieran chuckled. "You ladies didn't need to change out of your prairie dresses. You would've fit right in here."

"Maybe so," Dana said, as she unbuckled her seat-belt. "But long skirts aren't very practical or safe for running, jumping and climbing."

After exiting the car, Kieran removed the packed picnic basket from the backseat while Dana unbuckled Rosie. Then they went in search of an empty table near the playground.

They hadn't yet reached the grass when Rosie's breath caught and she slowed to a stop.

"Uh-oh." She pointed toward a small boy who'd just left the parking lot with his mom and was heading toward the playground. "That's the boy from Cowboy Fred's. The one who hit me."

She was right. Dana recognized both the child and his mother.

Kieran placed a hand on Rosie's shoulder, urging her to continue walking. "Let's go say hello."

"No." Rosie dug in her heels. "I don't want to. He was mean to me. He made blood come out of my nose, and it really hurt."

"Yes, I know," Kieran said. "But he told you he was sorry. Remember?"

Rosie looked up at him and frowned. "But what if he does it again?"

Dana cast a glance at "Uncle Daddy," who looked back at her and rolled his eyes. Then he urged the girl onward. "I'm sure he won't. Come on, princess. Let's go say hello."

As they started toward the swing set, each of its plastic seats shaped like a saddled merry-go-round horse, Rosie's steps slowed again. She turned to Kieran and frowned. "How come I have to talk to him?"

"In case you haven't noticed, most of the other kids on the playground are a lot older than you, and he's about your age. You'll probably become good friends—if you give each other a chance."

Dana looked over the girl's head at Kieran. When she caught his eyes, she pointed to her temple and mouthed, "Smart move."

He shot her a dazzling grin, his eyes as bright as the wild blue yonder, then placed the picnic basket on the grass. "I'll be back as soon as we bury the hatchet."

Rosie balked. "What's a hatchet?"

"Never mind," Kieran said. He glanced at Dana and shrugged, not quite able to stifle a grin. "Wish us luck, okay?"

Dana crossed her index and middle fingers to show him she was on his side and that she was hoping for the best.

He nodded, then took Rosie's hand. "Come on, princess. I'll face the dragon with you."

"But he's got a pirate shirt on today," Rosie said, as she reluctantly trudged along with him.

"You're right, but dragons and pirates won't stop a brave princess like you."

Dana followed them on their short trek to greet the mother and child.

"Hi, there," Kieran said to the towheaded boy. "Your name's Michael, right?"

The little guy nodded.

"Do you remember Rosie?" Kieran asked him. "We met you at Cowboy Fred's. And now here we are, ready to have a fun day at the park."

Michael bit down on his bottom lip and shot a careful peek at Rosie, who eyed him back. But neither uttered a word.

"It's nice to see you here." The mom looked down at her son and placed her hand on top of his head. "Isn't it, Michael?" Then she addressed Kieran and Dana. "We just moved to town, so we're still checking out places where we can play."

"I've lived in Austin my entire life," Kieran said, "but this is the first time I've ever come to this park. And that's really a shame, because I would have loved going down that sombrero slide—or riding on those horse swings. Maybe Michael and Rosie can show me how fast those ponies can go."

The boy brightened. "I can go *super* high and fast." Then he looked at Rosie. "You wanna do that, too?"

When she nodded, they both dashed off, with Kieran taking up the rear.

"It's nice to see a family together at the park," Michael's mother said. "Even before our divorce, Michael's dad rarely went on outings with us."

"Actually," Dana said, "We're not a family."

"I'm sorry. I just assumed you were."

It was an easy mistake to make, Dana supposed. She expected Michael's mother to quiz her further, but she didn't, which was a relief. She and Kieran had landed in an odd situation and a difficult one to explain, especially to a stranger.

"My son and I recently moved in with my parents," the woman said. "There aren't any families with young children in their neighborhood, so Michael doesn't have anyone to play with. I tried to enroll him in a preschool that's supposed to be a good one, but there's a pretty long waiting list. So I've tried to take him places where he can meet and play with other kids his age."

"You may not realize this," Dana said, "but there's a story hour at the library on Thursday mornings for preschoolers. You might try going there, too."

"That's a good idea." The woman laughed. "By the way, Mikey isn't the only one who needs to make new friends. My name is Elaine Wagner."

Dana took her hand, gave it a warm shake and introduced herself. "It's nice to meet you."

They both turned to watch the children play. But what really caught Dana's interest was Kieran, who would give one child's horse swing a push, then the next. It was such a fatherly thing for him to do, and knowing what she did about him, that he was a bachelor who didn't have any plans to settle down, it touched her heart.

"Is Rosie's father divorced?" Elaine asked.

There it was—the quiz Dana had been expecting.

Elaine undoubtedly found Kieran attractive—what woman wouldn't? And she probably wanted to learn whether he was available or not. Dana couldn't very well blame her for that. He was one sexy man, especially when he showed his Uncle Daddy side.

But Elaine had been open and forthcoming with Dana, so she figured it wouldn't hurt to answer honestly. "Rosie's father passed away recently, and since I was a family friend, I've been helping her and her guardian adjust to the changes in their lives."

"I'm so sorry," Elaine said. "Divorce isn't easy to explain to a child, but death must be worse."

Dana wanted to agree. As a child, she'd had a difficult time understanding why her parents had died and gone to heaven. Yet in spite of her grief and loneliness, she'd realized that they hadn't wanted to leave her behind. On the other hand, divorces were different.

"I'm sure some splits can get pretty nasty," Dana said, "which could be difficult for everyone involved."

"Ours was tougher on me. Michael's father never had been a big part of his life. He was always too busy for us."

"So he was a workaholic?" Dana asked, connecting the dots.

Elaine shielded her eyes from the sun's glare and looked at the playground, where the kids were swinging. "I assumed that he was because he used to spend so much time at the office. But I came to find out he had a special fondness for the attractive new receptionist."

Ouch. Now it was Dana's turn to sympathize. "I'm sorry to hear that."

"It was a big blow to my ego, that's for sure. But as it turned out, Mikey didn't seem to be too affected by it. It's not as if he'd had a *real* daddy to miss." Elaine continued to study her son, then added, "He does have a good grandpa, so that helps a lot."

About that time, Kieran returned to where the women stood and reached for the picnic basket that Dana had packed.

"We're going to have a picnic," she said to Elaine. "Why don't you and Michael join us? I have plenty of food."

"That's really nice of you to include us," Elaine said. "We ate a late breakfast before we came, so we won't eat much. I also brought some orange slices we can contribute, and I have a blanket in the car we can spread out on the grass."

"Then it looks like we're set." Dana glanced at the playground, which was about ten feet away, to check on the kids. They were just leaving the swing set and running toward the slide, both smiling.

"It looks like Michael and Rosie are well on their way to becoming friends," Dana said.

"I can see that." Elaine handed Dana a small bag,

then pointed toward her car. "If you'll keep an eye on the kids, I'll get that blanket from the trunk."

Minutes later, the two women had taken seats on top of the quilt they'd spread on the grass, the food set out between them. Kieran, who'd stretched out on the grass, drank a glass of lemonade Dana had brought.

While Dana and Elaine chatted, she soon learned that they had a lot in common, including a love of books and an interest in baking. If Kieran was bored with their conversation, he never let on. Instead, he studied a monarch butterfly that fluttered near the picnic basket.

About the time Dana thought they should call the children to come and eat, the boy and girl trotted back to the adults.

"I'm hungry," Rosie said. "Can we have a cookie?"

"After you eat a sandwich. But let's wash our hands first." Dana got to her feet, then walked with the children to the restrooms. Along the way, she listened to the newfound friends chattering away.

"My mommy is a good cooker," Michael said. "And sometimes, when she makes dinner, she lets me help."

"So does *my* mommy," Rosie said.

Dana's heart stalled. The poor little girl had never known her mother, and now she was creating an imaginary one to impress her new friend. She probably wanted to fit in and be like other children her age. Dana certainly knew that feeling. As a girl, she'd wished that she still belonged to a real family, one that didn't include foster parents.

"Me and my mommy made sugar cookies this morning," Rosie said. "I'll share one with you. But only after we eat."

Dana could hardly believe what just went down. Rosie implied that Dana was her mother, but Dana wouldn't correct her now. Not in front of Michael.

Then again, she didn't know how to address the issue at all. She'd read a few parenting articles, but that was a topic that hadn't come up.

"When it was my birthday," Michael said, "and when we lived at the other house that's far away, my mommy made cupcakes for the party. And I got to help put the frosting and little race cars on top."

"It's going to be my birthday," Rosie said. "My grandma said it's going to be in two weeks, and that's not very long to wait. I'm going to have a party, too. You can come, if you want to."

Dana wasn't sure what Sandra had told the child, but it was true. Her birthday was at the end of April— on the twenty-eighth, if she remembered correctly. But she doubted that Sandra had promised her a party. At least, not without talking it over with Kieran first.

That didn't mean Rosie wouldn't have one. Dana would make sure of it—one way or another.

That is, if Kieran wanted her help.

She glanced over her shoulder to where he sat on the grass, only to see him watching her and the children. Or was he more interested in her?

Oh, for goodness' sake. Talk about imagining things. A substitute mommy wasn't as bad as a nonexistent romance. And Kieran couldn't possibly be the least bit interested in her.

He was not only an heir to the Robinson technology dynasty, but he was a Fortune. And just because he'd hung out at the park this afternoon like an honest-to-goodness family man, didn't mean a thing. Nor did it mean that she should waste her time dreaming about things that would never come to be.

Chapter Nine

Kieran couldn't remember the last time he'd been on a picnic, let alone spent a couple hours at a park. And while he could think of a hundred other things he could be doing on a Saturday afternoon, like golfing with buddies or watching college baseball at his favorite sports bar, the day had actually turned out to be pleasant.

Now, as he drove back to Dana's house to drop her off, he wondered how to thank her for all she'd done for him and Rosie today. He'd mentioned his appreciation more than once, but that didn't seem to be enough.

There was something else he wanted to talk to her about, something that he couldn't mention in front of Rosie. Several times this afternoon, the little girl had called him Daddy, leaving off the Uncle. And to make matters even more complicated, he'd also heard her refer to Dana as her mommy.

Dana seemed to let it roll right off her back, which was probably the best approach. But Kieran thought he should address it, although he wasn't sure how.

Maybe he should talk it over with a child psychologist. Rosie might be missing her father—or longing for the kind of family most of the other children her age had. And there was nothing Kieran could do to fix that, no matter how badly he'd like to.

He glanced in the rearview mirror, where Rosie sat in her car seat, her eyes closed. Had she fallen asleep? She'd played hard today, so she had to be worn out.

"You know," Dana said, drawing him from his musing. "We...or rather *you*, should think about the upcoming *B-I-R-T-H-D-A-Y*."

He was going to ask who was having a birthday until he realized there was only one reason for Dana to spell the word.

"Should we plan a *P-A-R-T-Y*?" he asked.

"I think it's a good idea. And if you decide to go that route, I'd be happy to help."

"Thanks. I'll definitely take you up on that offer. I'll give you a call after we get home, when we're free to talk more about it." He took another peek at Rosie in the mirror. Her head was rolled to the side now, her lips slightly parted.

He supposed they could talk more now that Rosie appeared to be sleeping, but it might be best to give it some thought. And yes, that would give him an excuse to call Dana later. And not just to talk about the "Mommy and Daddy" stuff, but anything else that came up.

But when they pulled up into Dana's driveway and parked, he had a second thought and volunteered to carry the picnic basket inside for her.

"I've got it," she said. "It's practically empty now."

"Let me get it for you. I insist." Besides, that would give him the chance to talk with her privately on the porch. He'd still call Dana later, to talk about the party—or whatever.

Before he slid out of the car, he lowered the windows to make sure Rosie was comfortable. Then he removed the picnic basket from the backseat and carried it to the front porch, walking beside her.

"I'm not sure if you heard, but Rosie referred to me as her daddy more than once today. I had a feeling she was going to drop the *uncle* eventually."

"She lost her father recently, so I don't find it surprising that she considers you the next best thing." She slipped the key into the lock and turned to him. "Does that bother you?"

"In some ways. I don't want to take Zach's place in her heart. I want her to remember the man he was and the love he had for her. But that doesn't mean it doesn't please me at the same time. I guess it's complicated."

Dana reached out and stroked his arm, offering both comfort and understanding. "She's only three, Kieran. I know she's bright and will be turning four in a couple few weeks, but the chances of her remembering a whole lot about her father are slim. When was your first memory?"

She was right. He blew out a sigh. Then he set the basket aside, resting it on the small patio table near the door, and studied the woman he'd begun to rely on, the one he admired more than she'd ever know. The one who was not only stroking his arm but touching his heart.

"Did you hear her refer to you as her mommy?" he asked.

"A couple of times. Her grandma always filled that role for her, and right now, Sandra can't be there for her. I'm sure most of her friends at school have mothers, so it seems only natural that she'd try and create a family of her own, even if it's only imaginary."

"Are you okay with that?" he asked.

"This may sound weird to you, but it's actually a little flattering."

"I know what you mean." Kieran liked the fact that Rosie was willing to accept him as the next best thing to Zach.

"I'm sure she'll call me Dana again in time."

"You're probably right."

"The woman who eventually becomes her mommy is going to be a lucky lady," Dana said.

Had Zach lived, Dana might have become that lucky lady. Did she know that? Did she mourn for what might have been? She'd said—or implied—that she didn't. But that's just the kind of thing a loving, warmhearted woman like Dana would say to make things easier on those around her.

Kieran cupped her jaw, and their gazes met and locked. A rush of complicated emotions swirled up in his chest, threatening to wreak havoc on his life like a Texas twister. Yet it didn't scare him, even though it should.

"You're pretty special, Dana."

"So are you."

Unable to help himself, he slid his hand forward, from her jaw to the back of her neck, and drew her mouth to his.

He wouldn't have been surprised if she'd flinched or read him the riot act, but she leaned into him, slipped her arms around his neck and kissed him back—deeply and thoroughly.

It hadn't been all that long ago that he'd had the freedom to date whoever he wanted—and whenever. He'd had a fairly active sex life. But by the way his testosterone was pumping now, you'd think he hadn't had sex since his teen years.

Damn, he couldn't seem to get enough of her sweet vanilla taste, thanks in part to the sugar cookies they'd had for dessert. Nor could he breathe in enough of her classic scent.

As his arms tightened around her and she pressed her body close to his, his blood rushed through his veins, throbbing with intensity. If he wasn't careful, he'd make a scene right here on her front porch. Yet for a man who wasn't into public displays of affection, he didn't particularly care what her neighbors might think. And apparently, neither did she.

"Daaddy!" Rosie called out from the backseat of the car.

Caught with his hand in the proverbial sugar

cookie jar, Kieran tore his lips from Dana's and released her.

"I'm right here," he said, as if answering Rosie's call of Daddy. But he wasn't her father. Zach was.

Rosie rubbed her eyes and scrunched her face. "Were you kissing Mommy?"

Zach might have asked Kieran to step up and be Rosie's father, if the unthinkable happened. But he'd never asked him to take his place with Dana.

"It's not what you think," Kieran told her. "I'll be right there."

As he backed off the porch and stepped onto the lawn, he looked back at Dana and nodded toward his car. "I'd better take her home. I'll...talk to you later."

"Sure." Dana's voice came out so softly that he hardly heard her.

But if truth be told, he didn't want to talk to her about this now or later. Because, for the life of him, he had no excuse for what he'd just done.

Dana had no idea what had just happened.

Okay, she and Kieran had shared a heated kiss. And not just privately, but right outside her front door, where all the neighbors could see.

As far as she was concerned, the kiss had been amazing and so blood stirring it weakened her knees. Yet obviously it hadn't affected Kieran in the same way. But why would it?

Before taking custody of Rosie, the handsome bachelor could be seen every night at restaurants, concerts and galas all over town, a beautiful model or socialite on his arm. And no doubt, he probably woke up the next morning with her, too.

Dana wasn't a virgin, but she wasn't all that experienced, either. So while that kiss had been amazing, at least to her, Kieran clearly hadn't found it remarkable. In fact, he'd been so embarrassed or disappointed that he told Rosie she'd been mistaken, that she hadn't actually witnessed him and Dana in a lip lock.

For that reason, she'd been embarrassed and disappointed by the kiss, too. She'd put her heart and soul into it, but Kieran couldn't have rushed off any faster if his pants were on fire. So she must have done something wrong.

She scanned her yard as well as the sidewalk and street. Fortunately, there wasn't anyone in the vicinity who'd seen what'd just happened. As much as she'd like to have someone to talk to, to offer her advice, she was too new to the neighborhood to have made any friends or confidants. The only person she felt inclined to call was Monica, but she'd never liked sharing her humiliation with anyone, even her bestie.

She blew out an exasperated sigh. How could she have been so stupid as to think that she actually stood a chance with a man like Kieran Fortune Robinson?

There was no excuse, other than the fact that she was falling heart over brain for the guy and had made a real mess of things. The only thing she could do was tell him she was busy the next time he called asking for her help with Rosie.

Of course, watching him hightail it out of here

convinced her that he wouldn't be calling her any-time soon—if ever.

But in twenty minutes, she realized she'd been wrong about that when her cell phone rang and the caller ID told her it was Kieran.

She didn't want to answer, didn't want to talk about what had happened or what it all meant. With each ring, her heart skipped and fluttered until she thought it might stop completely.

Finally, she swallowed hard, cleared her throat and slid her finger across the screen, taking the call before the line disconnected.

"I'm sorry about ducking out so quickly," Kieran said.

She wasn't about to accept that lame apology, al-though she didn't expect more than that from him.

"That kiss took me by surprise," he added, a little chuckle fanning his words.

Apparently, he'd forgotten that he'd been the one to instigate it. So how could he have been taken aback by it? But there was no need to admit what she was really feeling. "Don't worry about it."

She could really go off on him and his quick de-parture, listing all the things he didn't have to worry about, but she let it go at that.

"I need to talk to you," he said. "And not on the phone."

"That's not necessary."

"Sure it is. How about dinner one of these nights? I'll find a sitter."

Like that was going to be an easy task for him to do, especially with Sandra's hands already full.

"I have a lot going on this week," Dana said.

He paused a moment, then pressed on. "How about next week?"

Now it was her turn for silence. "Listen, Kieran. I'm not interested in going out with you—as friends or as a teammate or…whatever. Kissing you was a big mistake and not one I plan on making again. So let's just pretend it didn't happen."

More silence. Then, "You're angry."

No, she was hurt. But since it was her fault for making assumptions, her anger was directed at herself. "Actually, I'm fine. And so are you. No harm, no foul."

"Yeah, well, I think there's more going on than you're admitting. Is it Zach?"

Why did he always bring up Zach? This was about Dana and the insecurities she claimed to have overcome but sometimes still battled, especially at times like this. But there was no way she'd bring that to the forefront of this conversation, so she tackled the one that was easier to admit. "Zach and I were never much more than friends. I can't even remember the last time he kissed me, so what does he have to do with it? Besides, he's gone and out of the picture. But I clearly made a mistake by kissing you, so don't worry. I'll never do it again."

A heavy silence filled the line until she wondered if she'd completely stumped him or if he'd hung up on her. Finally, he responded with a question. "What if I wanted you to do it again?"

She laughed, a short, choppy, insincere burble that mocked the tears filling her eyes. "Let's just forget it happened and get on with our lives. That's what I plan to do."

"What if I don't want you to?"

For a moment, she grasped for the hope he offered, the suggestion that he was actually feeling something for her. And while she'd give anything to have a family of her own, she knew better than to think it might carry the Fortune name. So she'd have to get over this and move on with her life. Because, if she didn't, she'd never stop battling those stupid, waifish insecurities.

"Goodbye, Kieran. I have something pressing to do." And that was true. She had to get off the phone before her voice broke, before she let him know how badly she hurt.

Then she disconnected the line and ended the call. Too bad she couldn't shut out the memory of his kiss as easily.

Kieran glanced at the cell phone in his hand. Dana had hung up on him. For a woman who'd kissed him as though she was staking a claim on him, she'd certainly cut him off just now.

What the hell had happened?

He redialed her number, then waited for her to answer. No one shut Kieran out like that. Her words didn't make a whole lot of sense, other than she'd pretty much indicated that she hadn't been thinking about Zach.

When she answered, instead of hello, she said, "What part of *goodbye* don't you understand?"

Wow. He'd really messed up, and he wasn't sure how to fix it.

"Listen, Dana. We need to talk. You already said no to dinner, but I think it would do us a world of good to clear the air. So maybe we can have a drink, a cup of coffee… Whatever. And I'd prefer to do it sooner, rather than later."

"There isn't anything to talk about."

"Yes, there is. You're angry—and maybe even hurt. And I'm not sure why. If it's because I came on to you so strongly, I'm sorry." Rather than tell her how he was feeling and how afraid he was to end things like this, he added, "I don't want to lose…whatever our friendship has become."

"You don't have to make things into something they're not. I forgive you for dashing off like you did. It's okay if you're not interested."

What was she talking about? Hell, he was incredibly attracted to her and had been fighting every one of his sexual urges.

"Okay, there's clearly been a big misunderstanding. Hell, I felt like a jerk all the way home. And now I'm feeling even worse."

At that, her voice softened. "It's not your fault— it's mine. I never should have read anything into that kiss."

He wasn't sure what she'd thought it all meant. Hell, he wasn't even sure himself. All he knew was that he wanted to take her out on a real date—and it sure as heck wouldn't be to Cowboy Fred's Funhouse and Pizza Emporium or a picnic at a park.

But should he push for that? What if she told him no?

Wow. This was surreal. He'd never worried about a woman turning him down since… Hell, he couldn't remember when. But he'd be damned if he'd accept Dana's refusal sitting down. Not when he suspected there was more going on than met the eye.

Did Dana have feelings for him? He suspected she might, because if she didn't, why would she have kissed him the way she had? And why would she be so angry and upset now?

"Please don't go anywhere. Just give me an hour. I'm coming to talk to you—and without Rosie."

Before she had time to object, he hung up the phone and called his sister Olivia.

When Olivia answered, feminine laughter erupted in the background.

"What's all that noise?" he asked.

"Zoe and Sophie are here, and we're helping Sophie with some wedding planning. May is just around the corner, so we don't have much time."

Sophie was going to marry Mason Montgomery, a computer programmer who also worked at Robinson Tech.

"It's funny you should call," Olivia said. "We were just talking about having Rosie be the flower girl. You don't have any objections, do you?"

"No, I'm sure she'll love that—especially if she can wear a princess gown."

"No problem there. We'll find the perfect dress for her to wear."

"Great. Just send me the bill." Kieran realized his

sisters were busy, but seeing as he had no other options, he told Olivia why he'd called. "I have a problem, and I need a big favor."

"What's that?"

"I need someone to watch Rosie for me this evening, and I hope that someone is you."

"Oh, no," Olivia said, laughing yet clearly serious, too. "I'm not a kid person. You ought to know that. But I'll provide you with a better option. Let me put Zoe on the line."

At this point, Kieran couldn't be choosy. And Olivia was right. Zoe would probably jump at the chance.

Once the phone had been transferred from one sister to the other, he restated his request.

"I'd be happy to watch her," Zoe said. "Where are you going?"

"I need to talk to a friend."

"A friend?" Zoe asked. "Male or female?"

"Does it matter?" he asked.

"Actually, it does. I can watch Rosie for an hour or two, but I have plans to meet some of my high school friends this evening. However, if you have a hot date, I'll adjust my plans."

Her response took him aback. "Why would you reschedule or cancel your plans for me if I'm seeing a woman?"

"Because I feel sorry for you. Instant fatherhood has probably put a real damper on your social life."

"You're right. Life as I once knew it has stalled altogether."

"So who is she?" Zoe asked, connecting dots he hadn't planned on revealing. "Anyone I know?"

"No. And it's really not that serious. It's just…well, I really need to talk to her." It was too soon to let his family think he might be feeling more for Dana than just friendship. Especially when he wasn't sure what to call it himself.

"Can you bring Rosie to Olivia's house?" Zoe asked.

"Of course. I can be there in half an hour. Is this going to interfere with your wedding discussions?"

"No, we'll be wrapping things up before you get here. Sophie will be leaving soon. She and Mason are going out to dinner tonight, and she needs to go home and get ready."

Kieran had planned to ask Sophie a question when he got there. But if she was leaving, he'd better do it now.

"Can you put Sophie on the phone?" he asked. "I'll only keep her a minute."

"Sure."

There was a murmur or two, then the sound of a chair moving across the floor. Finally Sophie got on the line and said, "Hi, Kieran."

"I have a question for you, Soph. Remember when Ariana Lamonte interviewed you for that article she was writing?"

"Yes, why?"

"She went to the history center the other day and seemed interested in some old magazine and newspaper articles about Dad."

"That makes sense. He started Robinson Tech shortly after moving to Austin. I'm sure she's just trying to get a few of her details straight."

Kieran had considered that. "Did anything strike you as odd about her or any of the questions she asked you?"

"No, not at all. Are you worried about something?"

"She's supposed to be writing about the 'new' Fortunes, which didn't bother me because a topic like that could end up being good publicity. But I think she might want to write an exposé about our old man."

"She seemed very sweet and sincere during my interview. I don't think she has any ulterior motives. Besides, with the half siblings who've turned up lately, I can't blame her for being curious about Dad."

"You're probably right. I'd better let you get back to your wedding plans. Tell Zoe and Olivia that Rosie and I are on the way."

After they ended the call, Kieran went into the living room, where he found Rosie playing with a puzzle. He helped her finish putting the pieces together to speed her along. After she chose a few toys and books to put in her backpack, he took her out to the car.

He stayed within the speed limit on the drive to Olivia's, but it wasn't easy. He was determined to get to Dana's house in time to take her to dinner.

Sure, there was always the possibility that Dana would refuse to go out with him, but there was something to be said for Kieran Fortune. He never took no for an answer.

* * *

If Dana had any sense at all, she'd leave the house before Kieran arrived. But she hadn't survived foster care and achieved all that she had today by running from uncomfortable situations, even if she found them downright embarrassing. So she kept herself busy by emptying the picnic basket and putting it away. She'd cleaned up the kitchen after she'd made cookies with Rosie, but she decided to do a more thorough job of it now.

To help keep her mind off Kieran, she turned on the radio to her favorite soft rock station. She loved listening to music from the 1980s and sometimes wished she'd been born thirty years earlier.

She just finished sweeping the floor—or actually, dancing with the broom—when the last chords of a James Taylor hit faded and the next song began.

As Rod Stewart sang the opening lyrics of "Have I Told You Lately," she turned off the radio. There'd be no professions of love today, even if they were only made by a singer. She'd no more than put the broom back in the closet when the doorbell rang.

Her heart pinged around in her chest like a pinball. It had to be Kieran. Was she up for this?

She'd have to be. And on the upside, once they had the talk he insisted upon having and put it behind them, her life would be back on track.

But the minute she opened the door and saw him standing on her porch, all sexy and handsome, she wondered if it was going to be as easy as she'd thought to not only put him out of her mind, but out of her life for good.

He offered her an easy grin. "I came to apologize again for ducking out on you like I did."

She didn't respond. Nor did she return his smile or invite him in. She did, however, scan the yard and look at the backseat of his car. "Where's Rosie?"

"With my sisters, Zoe and Olivia."

Clearly, he no longer needed Dana as a babysitter. That would make it easier to put an end to their friendship.

"I've been struggling with something," he admitted. "I have feelings for you, and I was afraid that it was too soon. Zach hasn't been gone that long, and you probably thought I was coming on too strong."

She placed her hands on her hips. "I told you before that I cared about Zach, but I'm not grieving for him in the way you think I am."

"Yeah, well, after that last kiss, I realized that had to be true." His smile deepened, dimpling his cheeks. But she still didn't return it.

She'd lost her head during that kiss, making a fool of herself, and she didn't need the reminder.

"I have no business getting involved with anyone," Kieran added. "Not when I'm solely responsible for Rosie. She's struggling with the loss of her father and a move from the only home she's ever known. I'm all she really has right now."

"I haven't asked anything of you."

"Yes, I know. And that's the point. You've been

great. And amazing. But if things turn in a romantic direction, it might not be fair to you."

"How so?"

"Rosie has to be my first priority, and the last thing in the world I want to do is hurt you."

"I'm a big girl. I have no intention of letting myself get hurt." Still, even though she'd heard those words coming out in her own voice, she wasn't sure she believed them.

Was she setting herself up for failure?

"I'm attracted to you, Dana. I didn't expect it to happen, but it did."

"You?" A man who could have almost any single woman in Austin? And he found *her* attractive? She slowly shook her head. "That's hard for me to believe."

"Then maybe this will help." He reached out, drew her into his arms and kissed her soundly, thoroughly and with more conviction than she'd ever thought possible.

As his tongue swept into her mouth, mating with hers, she lost all conscious thought. She clung to him, savoring the subtle taste of peppermint and his musky, mountain-fresh scent.

Yet in spite of a growing ache in her most feminine part, she broke the kiss long enough to lay her cheek against his and whisper, "We'd better take this inside. I don't want to provide a show for my neighbors or give them a reason to gossip."

Then she took his hand, drew him into the house and closed the door. Their conversation probably should have continued at that point, but when he opened his arms, she stepped back into his embrace and raised her lips to his.

As the kiss deepened, primal need took over. Her hands explored him, caressed and stroked him, as his did her, until desire threatened to explode. But it wasn't just passion stealing Dana's thoughts and better judgment. Her heart had become fully engaged, too.

That really ought to concern her, and undoubtedly it would once she came back to her senses. If she ever did,

Before she could consider that thought, Kieran's cell phone rang, interrupting the sweet bliss. And Dana was torn between hoping he'd ignore the call and needing a moment to catch her breath.

She opted for breathing and allowing her brain the chance to gather her thoughts. "You'd better answer that."

"Yeah, probably so. But I'd rather not." Still, he reached for his phone and swiped the screen.

Moments later, he glanced at Dana and gave a slight roll of his eyes, then continued the conversation with whoever had called. "No, you're not bothering me. What's wrong?"

He listened a moment. "She's got to be exhausted after a day at the park. And she only had about a five-minute nap. She's probably having a meltdown, but I'll be right there."

After disconnecting the line, he looked at Dana, his lips forming a frown. "I have to go, but I intend to finish this later. What are you doing tomorrow night? Can we have dinner?"

"What about a sitter?"

"I'll find someone."

Dana smiled. "That little meltdown might mean that your sisters aren't going to be an option next time."

"Then I'll call Kelly or one of the other girls. You and I still need to discuss what to do about this."

By *this*, he meant the sexual attraction that had increased to astronomical proportions, at least as far as Dana was concerned.

"Let's take things slowly," she said, wanting to guard her heart.

"Sure. We'll keep things simple and uncomplicated."

She nodded, then watched him leave. Rather than follow him out to the car, she stayed inside. He might want to keep things simple, but for her, simple had left the station a long time ago.

Chapter Ten

As luck would have it, Kieran had no more than picked up Rosie from Olivia's and started the drive to his own house when the tired little girl drifted off to sleep.

He was actually getting used to being a stand-in daddy and even enjoyed it at times. But having to cancel plans, especially those that were romantic in nature, was definitely one of the downsides of parenthood or guardianship. And the plans he'd made while kissing Dana had been both romantic and major.

He'd meant what he'd said about taking things slowly, even though his hormones had argued otherwise just minutes ago. But it seemed that he and Dana were finally on the same page—and on the right track. So at least he could head home with a smile and hope for a brighter future.

He'd just pulled up to his building when his cell phone rang. He glanced at the screen displayed on his dash and saw that it was Sandra calling. He answered quickly, trying to keep the apprehension from his tone.

Thankfully, her response was light and upbeat. "How are things going?" she asked.

Better, now that Rosie had finally dozed off. But having the night end before it had a chance to get off the ground had been disappointing, although he wasn't about to complain to Sandra.

"We're doing just fine," he said. "We spent the afternoon at the park with Dana. Rosie met a new friend, and now she's asleep in the backseat. How are you doing? Is Sam feeling any better?"

"Yes, he is. The meds seem to be working. He's eating better, getting plenty of rest and gaining strength. So the doctor is pleased."

"That's good to hear."

"Anyway," Sandra said, "the reason I called was to talk to you about Rosie's birthday."

"Dana mentioned something to me earlier today, although we didn't discuss it. What did you have in mind?"

"I'd like to host the party here at the ranch—if that's all right with you. It's close to her preschool and the church, so most of her friends live nearby."

"That might be a good idea, but I don't want you to go to any trouble."

"It'll actually be fun for me," Sandra said. "And I promise not to go to any extra work. I can have

Kelly and her friends come that day and chase after the kids. And, of course, you and Dana can take part, too—if you want to."

Kieran laughed. "You strike a hard bargain, Sandra."

"Then you're okay with having it at the Leaning L?"

"As long as you'll let me and Dana do most of the work."

"Oh, good. Some of the parents like to host those parties at places like Cowboy Fred's because it's less work for them. But their food isn't very good. So I'd rather do the cooking. I'll keep it simple and pace myself, so don't worry about it being stressful."

Kieran had eaten enough meals at the Leaning L to know that he'd much rather eat anything Sandra made than Cowboy Fred's crappy pizza.

"I have one other question for you," Sandra said. "I'd like to have Rosie spend the night tomorrow so we can talk about her party and what she'd like. I already talked to Kelly, and she's available for a slumber party. Is that okay with you?"

Kieran didn't have to ponder the decision very long, since that would allow him to take Dana out— if she'd agree to go with him. "I'm sure Rosie would love to spend the night with you. What time do you want me to drop her off?"

"How about four o'clock?"

"Perfect." That gave him time to go home and shower before picking up Dana. "We'll see you tomorrow."

As soon as the call ended, Kieran dialed Don Ramon's, a classy restaurant that not only offered some of his favorite Mexican dishes, like tacos and enchiladas, but also served trendy Southwestern fare and boasted a full tequila bar that was the best this side of the Rio Grande.

When he got them on the line, he requested a table for two on the patio.

"Seven o'clock would be great," he told the woman taking his call.

His plan to take Dana out tomorrow night was coming together nicely.

Sitter? Check.

Dinner reservations? Check.

Beautiful woman to accompany him? Still pending. But he wasn't worried.

Should he order flowers? That might be a nice touch. One way or another, he would make this date extra special—and a night Dana would never forget.

Dana hadn't planned to go out with Kieran this evening, but when he'd shown up at her front door holding a bouquet of long-stem yellow roses and wearing a dashing grin, her resolve to avoid getting romantically involved with him had crumbled.

So now here she was, sitting across a linen-draped pation table with Kieran at Don Ramon's, one of Austin's finest—and probably most expensive—Mexican restaurants.

Kieran lowered his heavy, leather-bound menu. "If you like seafood, the camarones rancheros is good."

"I was thinking about having chili rellenos," she said. "Although there are a couple of chicken dishes that are pretty tempting."

"All the food here is good. You won't be disappointed with anything you choose."

He'd obviously been here many times, and probably with a date. Yet that didn't dull Dana's pleasure at being here with him. The man certainly knew how to treat a lady. He'd made Dana feel special from the moment he'd handed her the fragrant bouquet of roses. And in the car, he'd set the mood with soft jazz playing on Sirius. The royal treatment continued when the valet opened her car door and when Kieran brought her inside.

In the background, near a tree adorned with twinkly little white lights, a mariachi band played an array of Spanish romantic ballads. She didn't understand a word that they sang, but the music cast an amorous ambiance in the room, especially when they moved to their table and gave them a private serenade.

Was she really on an actual date with Kieran Fortune?

She was tempted to pinch herself. Instead, she opted to settle in and enjoy the handsome man's company.

One of the service staff placed a bowl of tortilla chips on their table, along with salsa fresco and guacamole.

"Thanks, Pablo." Kieran reached for one of the

chips and raised it in the air. "They make everything fresh, including the tortillas."

She wasn't surprised. The decor alone—with the white plastered walls and dark wood beams as well as an artistic mural depicting historical life in Old Mexico—was enough to convince her that this wasn't your run-of-the-mill restaurant.

"I'm not sure if you like guacamole or salsa," Kieran said, "but Don Ramon's has the best I've ever tasted."

"It's funny," she said. "I don't like avocados, but I love guacamole. One day, I was having dinner at my friend Monica's house. Her *abuelita*—her grandmother—had prepared a Mexican feast for us and encourage me to taste her special recipe. I did and was surprised at how good it was."

He dipped his chip into the guacamole, then handed it to her. "Try this and tell me if there's any comparison."

She took a bite and had to agree. "This is a little different, but I think it's just as good."

Her thoughts drifted back to the day Abuelita had prepared that amazing dinner, when Dana had felt a part of Monica's entire family. All she'd ever wanted was to be accepted and loved by people who knew her best.

When the waiter had finished pouring glasses of red wine, Kieran lifted his in a toast. "To our first evening out."

Dana clinked her glass against his. If this was their

first evening, then Kieran expected there would be others. She certainly was game, if he was.

After placing their orders, they settled back and enjoyed their wine, which had a hint of cranberry. With a candle softly burning and the mariachis playing, the evening had turned incredibly romantic.

But maybe that was due to the handsome man across the table from her. And for some reason, she had the feeling that the night would only get better with each minute that passed.

She was right.

By the time Kieran was driving her home, her heart rate was soaring and the heat was building. She lifted her long hair off her neck, refusing to give any thought to why she'd worn it down tonight. Still, she couldn't stop one thought from echoing in her mind. When he dropped her off, would he try to kiss her again?

She certainly hoped he would. And if he didn't? Would she be bold enough to take the lead?

When they pulled up at her house, she was reluctant to see the night end. "Would you like to come in for a cup of coffee? Or a glass of wine?"

He tossed her a dazzling, bright-eyed smile. "I'll have whatever you're having."

They got out of the car and walked to the door. Her fingers trembled when she pulled the keys from her purse, and it took longer than she'd expected to slip them into the lock.

Once inside the house, she said, "It'll only take a minute to put on a pot of coffee."

"Do you need any help?"

"No, I've got this." What she didn't have was any idea where this night would go. But she was up for the adventure.

She left him in the living room, then headed into the kitchen. Her hands trembled again as she filled the carafe with water and the basket with ground coffee beans, especially when she heard music playing—something soft and slow.

Kieran must have turned on her television to the music station. She hadn't told him to make himself at home, but she was glad that he had. While the coffee brewed, she returned to the living room, where Kieran stood in the center of the floor.

He reached out a hand to her. "Do you want to dance?"

Her heart scrambled to right itself, as heat and desire warred with her common sense—and her pride. Kieran had acquired a lot of practice over the years and was surely a good dancer. But she'd... Well, it's not like she had two left feet or didn't enjoy dancing. Just ask her broom!

A giggle nearly burst free, but she bit it back. In spite of her momentary nervousness, she stepped forward and into his embrace.

Kieran pulled her close, and she leaned into him, swaying with the music, caught up in his musky scent, the strength of his arms, the magic of his touch.

She realized that he'd only used the music as an excuse for him to hold her, but she didn't care. He was an ace at seduction, but she refused to think about the other women he'd charmed. Not when she wanted to take whatever he had to offer her tonight.

As their bodies pressed together, they stroked and caressed each other. His hand slid up her side, the fabric of her black dress moving with it. When he cupped her breast, kneading it, his thumb skimmed her nipple and sent her senses reeling.

He was way too good at this, which probably ought to concern her, at least a little bit. But she couldn't help her desire for more.

Did she dare mention it?

Did she even need to?

His breath was warm and moist as he trailed kisses along her neck. She leaned her head back, granting him better access. She was clay in his hands, and he was the master artist. Yet he brought her to life in so many ways, making her bolder than she'd ever known she could be.

She'd lost count of the number of songs that played, although it might only have been three, each one more romantic than the last. All the while, they'd kissed and stroked each other until she thought she'd melt in a puddle on the floor.

Why wasn't he pressing her for more?

Because he didn't have to. She drew away, her breathing soft yet ragged, and said, "I invited you in for coffee, and it's probably ready. But I'm tempted to suggest another after-dinner alternative."

"Like I said…" He smiled, his eyes laden with passion. "I'll have whatever you're having."

She nodded, then reached for his hand and led him to her bedroom. "I don't think either of us needs a caffeine boost."

"I don't," he said. Then he took her back into his arms and began kissing her all over again.

She wasn't entirely sure where this was going, but she had a pretty good idea. She might regret this in the morning, but for now, she would enjoy every moment.

Things were turning out just the way Kieran had hoped they would. He'd be lying if he didn't admit he wanted to make love to her, but he didn't know how Dana felt. She certainly surprised him by taking him into her bedroom.

He barely noticed the antique oak bed. All he really saw was Dana. He kissed her again—long and deep. His hands slid along the curve of her back and down the slope of her hips. He pulled her hips forward, against his erection, and she arched forward, revealing her own need, her own arousal. Another surge of heat rushed through him.

Had he ever wanted a woman this badly? Right this moment, he sincerely doubted it. The quiet, dignified librarian was turning out to be even more amazing and breathtaking than he'd thought. If a man wasn't careful, he might be tempted to give up the footloose life of a bachelor and do something new, commit to someone special. Someone like Dana.

When she drew her lips from his, then slowly turned around, she swept her hair to the side like a veil, revealing the zipper for him. He pulled it down, slowly and deliberately. Then he peeled the fabric from her shoulders, taking his time to kiss every inch of the skin he uncovered.

She made a soft sound, almost a whimper, then turned to face him. Her gaze never left his as she let the dress slip to the floor.

He marveled at the sight of her, standing before him in a lacy black bra and a matching pair of skimpy panties. For some reason, he'd expected her to wear conservative underwear, but that was yet another amazing revelation for him. As she'd slowly exposed layer after layer of the real Dana to him, he couldn't wait to see what other surprises awaited him.

Her body, slender and lithe, was sexier and even more perfect than he'd imagined it to be. And tonight, she belonged to him.

Following her lead, he unbuttoned his shirt and tossed the custom-made garment to the side like a cheap suit. Next he unbuckled his belt and undid his slacks.

When he'd removed all but his boxer briefs, she skimmed her nails across his chest, setting off a rush of need throbbing in his veins. Then she unsnapped her bra and freed her breasts, full and round, the tips peaked and ready to be loved.

As he bent and took a nipple in his mouth, she gasped in pleasure. He laved first one breast, and then the other with kisses until they were both fully aroused.

He lifted her in his arms and placed her on top of

the bed. Her red hair splayed upon the white pillow sham, her lovely body awaiting him on top of the white down comforter.

Determined to make sure she wouldn't have a single regret in the morning, he joined her on the bed, where they continued to kiss, to taste and to stroke each other until they were both breathless with need.

"We have all night," she said, as she pulled free of his embrace and removed the remainder of their clothes. "So we can take things slow and easy later. Right now I need to feel you inside of me."

He didn't want to prolong the foreplay any longer, either. And she was right. They had the rest of the night.

About the time he was going to reach for his pants to get the condom he always carried with him, she rolled to the side of the bed, opened the nightstand drawer and pulled out a small, unopened box of condoms.

He wasn't sure if she kept them handy just in case, or whether she'd planned for this night to happen. Either way, he was glad she'd been prepared.

Taking the packet she offered him, he tore it open and rolled on the condom. Then, as he hovered over her, she reached for his erection and guided him right where she wanted him to be.

He entered her slowly at first, but as her body responded to his, he increased the tempo. They moved together in a primal dance, taking and giving until they reached the peak together.

Her breath caught as she climaxed, and her nails

pressed into his shoulders as she let go. He shuddered, releasing with her in a head-spinning, heart-searing sexual explosion that begged to be repeated throughout the night.

He'd gone without sex for a while, which might be why tonight had been so incredibly good...

Oh, hell. Who was he kidding? In his heart of hearts, he knew it was because of Dana. And he feared what might be happening to them. To *him*.

He'd told her that they'd take things slowly, but that's not what had just happened. They'd taken a wild ride to the stars and beyond, and as he lay in a stunning afterglow, he thought that he might never want to leave Dana's arms or the peace and comfort he'd found in her bed.

And that's just the reason he needed to. Making love with her had been anything but casual or simple. It had all the earmarks of love and promises of forever—something that scared a dedicated bachelor like him spitless.

Still, he rolled to the side, taking her with him— as was his custom after lovemaking. But tonight had been different. Dana was different.

For that reason alone, he had to escape before he said something he might regret, made promises he didn't dare make.

But how did a conscientious lover who'd just had the best sex of his life with a woman who'd intrigued him like no other tell her that he had to leave? That he wouldn't be spending the night?

* * *

Wrapped in Kieran's arms, Dana basked in the afterglow of a stunning climax, afraid to move or even blink for fear she'd wake up from this beautiful dream.

She'd just had the most stunning evening of her life, followed by the best sexual experience she'd ever had. And in spite of her reluctance to get involved with a man who lived in a completely different world than hers, she'd fallen hopelessly in love with Kieran Fortune.

She couldn't very well tell him, though. It was too soon, and it might scare him off. So now what? She'd instinctively known what to do just moments before, when they were kissing and caressing, but she was completely stymied now.

Should she invite him to spend the night with her? Or was that a given?

If she'd had more experience with this sort of thing, she'd know exactly how to handle it. But she was such a novice, and Kieran had just raised the learning curve to an unbelievable height.

He pressed a kiss on her brow, his lips lingering as he said, "That was amazing."

She smiled, relieved that she wasn't the only one who'd come to that conclusion. "I thought so, too."

He trailed his fingers along her shoulder and down her arm, sending tiny tingles dancing on her skin. "As much as I hate to leave, I have to go."

No, you don't, she wanted to say. *Stay with me. Forever.* But her self-esteem, which had grown strong after college graduation, had just taken an unexpected hit and now floundered.

"I need to pick up Rosie at the Leaning L bright and early in the morning," he added.

That sounded like a lame excuse. Why couldn't he set the alarm for four or five and then leave from her house? She would gladly wake up with him and send him off with a kiss and a cup of freshly brewed coffee.

She would have suggested that option, but she didn't want to come across as clingy or needy.

"I'd hate to arrive at the ranch wearing the same shirt and pants that I dropped Rosie off in. That would set off suspicion about where I spent the evening—as pleasant as it's been."

That made sense, she supposed. She wasn't ready for the world to know how she was feeling, or what they'd done, either. But one day soon, she hoped to shout it from the proverbial mountain tops.

He pressed a second kiss upon her brow, then climbed out of bed and proceeded to pick up his discarded clothes. For a man who was always stylishly dressed, his shirts neatly pressed, he did look a little mussed.

He cast a smile at her. "You look beautiful lying there. So there's no need to walk me to the door."

No way would she do that. She rolled out of bed, still as naked as the day she was born. "There's coffee in the kitchen, and it's still fresh. I'll pour it in a to-go cup to take with you."

"That'd be great. Thanks." The warm smile he

wore suggested that she hadn't just experienced a bout of hit-and-run sex.

After snagging her robe from the closet, she padded to the kitchen. Then she removed a thermal cup from her cupboard, filled it with coffee and carried it to the living room, where Kieran was preparing to leave.

A small inner voice rose to the surface, threatening to cry out, *Please don't go*. But she stifled it with a smile. "Thank you for dinner. And…everything."

"I'll call you tomorrow." He took her in his arms and gave her a sweet, lingering goodbye kiss. "And I promise to look for a dependable sitter. I'd rather not wait too long before…doing this again."

She practically wilted in his arms. Okay, so he wasn't just giving her a brush-off.

"We said we'd take things slowly," she said, her ego gaining strength once more.

"That's for the best."

She nodded and offered him a send-off smile, suggesting she was in complete agreement. And she was. Taking things one day at a time was the smart thing to do, the right thing.

Still, a wisp of disappointment swirled around her as she watched him open the door and let himself out.

He said he'd call. And he'd implied there'd be other nights like this, so she had no choice but to believe him. She'd cling to that promise, knowing it was the best she'd get from him for now.

Making love with Kieran had been out of this

world, but had it been good enough for an experienced bachelor like him?

Time would tell, she supposed.

Either way, tonight's memory would last her a lifetime.

Chapter Eleven

Kieran had worried that, after their lovemaking, Dana would expect more from him than he was prepared to give. But that hadn't been the case. She'd given him plenty of space in the following days and hadn't asked anything of him.

In fact, each time they'd talked on the phone, he'd been the one to place the call. For that reason alone, he'd found himself more drawn to her than ever. And stranger still, he felt compelled to push for more of her time.

They hadn't seen each other since they'd made love last week, something he hoped to remedy soon.

Today, after leaving Robinson Tech, he stopped by the post office, where he had a PO box, to pick up his mail. Then he picked up Rosie at preschool and headed home.

All the while, Rosie chattered about her upcoming birthday. "All my friends are gonna come on Saturday, even Teddy."

Kieran had never heard that child's name. Maybe it was a new child at school who'd moved up on the waiting list. "Is Teddy a new boy at school?"

Rosie laughed. "Teddy isn't a *boy.* He's a dog. And he's really cute. He comes to the fence when we're on the playground. He's a little dirty, but he's really nice. And when you poke your finger through the hole, he licks it."

Kieran would have to talk to one of the teachers and ask what the school was doing about strays that roamed near the vacant field behind the playground. Slobbery dog kisses on fingers didn't sound very sanitary to him. And what about bites?

"So can Teddy come to my party?" she asked. "We have to pick him up in our car."

"I'm sure Teddy already has plans for that day." Kieran glanced in the rearview mirror and caught Rosie frowning at him.

She slowly shook her head. "No, that's not true. Teddy doesn't have a family. And he's lonely. That's why Miss Peggy called the dog catcher to take him to a special place where he could find a new home."

"Sounds like your teacher had a good plan."

"Yes, but when the man came to get him, Teddy got scared and ran away. So I told Miss Peggy that we could keep him because our house is big, and our family is small. We have room for one more."

"You have a point," Kieran said. "But I'm not allowed to have pets in this building."

"I got a good idea," Rosie said. "There's room for all of us at the ranch. We could all live there, like me and my other daddy did. And then Teddy could be my dog."

"You'll have to talk to your grandparents about that," Kieran said. "I mean about Teddy living there. We already have a home. But you can visit the ranch as often as you want."

"Okay, I'll ask Grandma. But she'll say yes because she likes dogs."

Kieran pulled into the underground parking garage and steered into his assigned space. After he got Rosie out of her car seat, he took her by the hand, walked to the elevator and rode up to their unit on the tenth floor.

"Can Dana come over tonight?" Rosie asked.

That invitation had been at the top of Kieran's to-do list. "We'll have to call and invite her."

"Can I do it?"

"Sure. When we get inside, I'll dial her number for you."

Moments later, Kieran whipped out his cell phone and called Dana. As he listened to each ring, his pulse escalated, reaching a peak when she finally answered.

"Hey," he said. "Rosie and I had an idea, and she'd like to talk to you."

"Sure, put her on."

As soon as he handed over his cell, Rosie started the conversation with the dinner invitation, which he assumed Dana accepted, because the little girl's face broke into a huge grin. Then she immediately launched into a full report of everything that had happened that day at school, starting with apple slices for midmorning snack and a story about a purple whale.

He let her jabber while he sorted through the mail. Power bill, alumni association newsletter and dental appointment reminder. He was just about to set it all on the stack of things that needed his attention when he realized he'd been negligent and had let things pile up.

So he crossed the room to the kitchen desk and went through each item, noting the due dates. At the bottom, he spotted the wedding invitation he'd received a while back. It was addressed to Mr. Kieran Fortune Robinson and Guest.

He set the other things aside and opened it.

Mr. and Mrs. Gerald Robinson
request the honor of your presence
at the marriage of their daughter

Sophie Anne
to
Mason Montgomery

Saturday, the sixth of May
at six o'clock in the evening
The Driskill Hotel ballroom

With the wedding just around the corner, his sisters would want his RSVP as soon as possible. So he pulled out the response card, opened the drawer and pulled out a pen. His right hand hovered a moment over the line where he was to provide the number who'd be attending.

Dana immediately came to mind, since she was the only woman in the world he'd consider taking. But he'd made it a point never to take a date to family events. And while he was sorely tempted to make an exception this time, it was too soon.

Besides, his sisters already had visions of him running off in the moonlight with a special lady. Why fuel their imaginations?

"Daddy!" Rosie called out. "Mommy wants to talk to you!"

Great. That cinched it. All he needed was for Sophie's flower girl to refer to Dana and him as her mom and dad. He'd never hear the end of it. So he gripped the pen tightly and marked a big, solid *1* on the line and then wrote his name. Before he could place the small card into the its envelope, Rosie called out again, "Hurry, Daddy! She wants to know if she should bring dinner. And she also said it was okay if Teddy comes to my party! She said she will bring him if he doesn't have a ride."

Kieran rolled his eyes. He'd have to let Dana know that Sammy wasn't a child before she made him a party favor and put him on the guest list. "I'll be right there, Rosie."

Then he hurried into the living room, pumped that he'd get to see Dana again tonight.

Dana tried to tamp down both her excitement and nervousness while driving to Kieran's house. She was glad that she'd been invited to dinner—and that she'd been told not to bring a thing but herself.

It was especially nice that the invitation had come from both Kieran and Rosie. She'd been a little worried about him leaving her house so quickly after they'd made love, but she'd probably expected too much. He'd mentioned taking things slowly, and... well, now here they were, moving right along.

As much as she looked forward to having some time alone with Kieran after Rosie went to sleep, the focus during the early hours would be on Rosie's birthday party. The little girl wanted a princess theme and, after talking to Sandra on the phone, Dana was determined to make that wish come true.

According to Sandra, Kelly and her friends wanted to decorate the ranch house like a castle. So Dana had gone shopping after work yesterday and picked up party favors, plus tiaras for the girls and crowns for the boys.

Since Dana had volunteered to make the cake, she'd researched various internet sites and found the perfect design, which was similar to one her mother had made her when she was six. To make the three-dimensional "princess," she'd make a cake in a bundt pan, which would form the gown. She'd already purchased a Barbie doll to place in the hole. Then she'd frost the cake and the doll's bodice with pink frosting and decorate it with edible crystals and sparkles. Rosie would love it.

Since that cake wouldn't be enough to feed everyone Rosie had invited, including Michael and his mother, Elaine Wagner, Dana was going to make cupcakes, each one decorated as a flower, that would surround the princess.

Needless to say, Dana was nearly as excited about the party as Rosie was. She could hardly wait for Saturday.

Even more exciting was the evening that awaited her at Kieran's.

After parking her car in a guest spot under his building, she greeted the doorman, who'd not only expected her arrival but called her by name. And that was another sign that she and Kieran were on the right track. Then she took the elevator to his tenth-floor apartment and rang the bell.

A happy Rosie met her at the door, which warmed her heart. But it was the dashing man in the background who nearly took her breath away and sent her thoughts soaring to dreamland.

Rosie reached for Dana's hand and pulled her inside. "I'm glad you finally got here. We *missed* you."

She glanced over the child's head once more, her gaze meeting Kieran's. Her eyes asked the question she couldn't voice. *Did we?*

His wink was the only answer she needed.

"And we have pizza," Rosie added. "It's not the

yucky kind from Cowboy Fred's. We found another place that cooks it better."

"I don't care what we eat," Dana said. "I'm just glad that we all get to have dinner together."

What she didn't mention was that she'd brought a toothbrush and a change of clothes with her—just in case she was also invited to spend the night.

Since she hadn't wanted to appear presumptuous or eager, she'd packed them in a gym bag, which seemed like something she might keep in the trunk of her car for a spur-of-the-moment workout—rather than a planned sleepover.

After all, they'd agreed to take things slow.

When Kieran walked over and took her hand, he looked and smelled so good that she needed a mental reminder. *The operative word is* slow, she repeated to herself. But looking at him, she couldn't help wanting to move things along a little faster.

"Come on into the kitchen," Kieran said. "We should eat while the pizza is still warm. Can I get you a glass of wine?"

"Just half a glass," she said. "I have to drive home."

"You got it," he said, as if a sleepover had never crossed his mind. Then he withdrew a bottle from a small wine cooler near the desk area. "I have a Napa Valley merlot I think you'll like."

She tamped down the minor disappointment. "Sounds good."

Minutes later, they sat at the kitchen table, a glossy black, ultramodern piece with matching chairs, to eat the cheese pizza. It was actually delicious. And so was the vegetarian antipasto salad, which had a tasty vinaigrette dressing.

"Guess what?" Rosie set down her glass, the milk leaving a white mustache on her upper lip. "I get to be the flower girl when Sophie and Mason get married. I'm going to walk in first and drop roses on a rug for the bride to step on. And I get to wear a real princess dress and a flower crown on my head."

"How fun!" Dana told the child. Then she looked at Kieran. "When's the wedding?"

"Saturday, May sixth. It'll be in the ballroom at the Driskill Hotel."

Why wasn't she surprised? Talk about dream wedding locales, at least in Dana's mind. The landmark hotel had been built in 1886 by cattle baron Jesse Driskill and had been providing its guests with luxury accommodations for more than a hundred and thirty years.

"I'll bet the wedding will be beautiful," Dana said. And expensive. The cheapest rooms had to cost at least three hundred dollars a night. But then, a fancy place like that was to be expected for the wedding of a Fortune.

Kieran didn't respond, so she let it go. What she wouldn't give to go as his plus one.

Once they finished the pizza, Kieran told Rosie it was time to put on her pajamas and get ready for bed. But the girl objected. "I want to wear my princess jammies, and they're in the laundry."

"Actually, they're in the dryer. I'll get them for

you." Kieran glanced at Dana. "Don't worry about the mess. I'll be right back."

Dana wasn't about to just sit there, waiting for him to return. So she cleared the table and put the dishes in the sink. She put the leftover pizza slices in plastic bags, then placed them in the fridge. Next, she folded the empty box and took it to the recycle bin, which was located near the kitchen desk.

She couldn't help noticing the elegant invitation spread out on top. In formal script, it was addressed to *Mr. Kieran Fortune Robinson and guest*.

Just imagining herself going to the Driskill Hotel on Kieran's arm shot a combination of excitement and nervousness clean through her.

What would she wear? She might have several dresses hanging in her closet, but none of them would be appropriate for a Fortune wedding. She'd have to go shopping—and not at the usual places she frequented. An event that classy and special would require a trip uptown. Her budget would take a hit, but she'd make it work.

She scanned the invitation. May 6 wasn't that far away. She'd need to schedule a hair appointment, too.

As she put the invitation down, her eyes lit on the matching response card which lay next to a pen. She assumed he was getting ready to mail his RSVP. But her heart clenched and her tummy twisted when she saw a big *1* where she'd hoped she'd see a *2*.

"Thanks for cleaning up," Kieran said, as he returned to the kitchen.

Dana slowly turned around. Aching with disappointment, the words rolled out of her mouth before she could give them a second thought. "You're not taking a guest to your sister's wedding?"

He cleared his throat, as if the question had taken him aback and he needed a moment to form a reply. "I thought about it, but I decided it was better if I didn't. I've never taken a date to family events. For one thing, I know what they'd assume, and I don't want anyone jumping to conclusions."

"That would be terrible, wouldn't it?"

"Not exactly *terrible*," he said. "But I'm not ready to give anyone reason to speculate."

And sadly, Dana had been speculating all evening.

How could she have been so stupid? She'd known full well going into this thing that she couldn't compete with any of the women Kieran usually dated. And she'd never fit into his social circles.

Was she destined to always miss the mark when it came to finding Mr. Right? If so, she'd never be able to create a family for herself.

"You're not upset, are you?"

Upset? No. She was crushed. And angry. But mostly at herself. Yet there was no way she'd let him know any of that. "Actually, I'm busy that day anyway."

As luck would have it, Rosie came trotting back into the kitchen in her pajamas and bunny slippers. "Will you read me a story, Mommy?"

At the sound of that word, her heart clenched. The other times Rosie called her Mommy she warmed to the name, but tonight it chilled her. She wasn't

Rosie's mommy, and she never would be. And what about Kieran? He seemed to be so concerned about his family getting the wrong impression about his relationship with Dana. But what about Rosie?

Dana knelt down, wrapped her arms around the vulnerable little girl and kissed her. "I'd love to, honey. But I have something important I need to do this evening. I only had time for pizza, and now I have to leave."

"When are you coming back?" the child asked.

"One day soon," Dana said, glad she didn't have a nose like Pinocchio's, which would be a foot long now. Then she headed for the living room, where she'd left her purse.

For some crazy reason, she actually expected Kieran to stop her, but he just let her walk out the door as if she'd never belonged there in the first place.

The moment Dana left Kieran's house on Wednesday night and shut the door, guilt slammed into him. And so did a sense of loss. At first, he'd tried to convince himself that letting things cool off between them was for the best.

At one time, he'd enjoyed a single, unencumbered life. If one of the women he dated even hinted that she might want a commitment, he'd almost have an allergic reaction. But after a few days without seeing Dana or even talking to her on the phone, the remorse had really set in. And by Saturday morning, before leaving for Rosie's party at the ranch, he'd had to admit that he'd not only reacted like a jerk, but he'd also been a fool. He was going to have to apologize, and hopefully, she'd forgive him. Something told him she would. Then, once the party was over, he'd invite her over for dinner—and then he'd ask her to spend the night.

But making things right with his lover wasn't the only reason he wanted to get to the ranch early. He'd promised Sandra he'd help. She'd always been a conscientious hostess, and he didn't want her to overdo it trying to please people today.

She was also an excellent housekeeper, and he suspected she hadn't been able to keep up with her usual tasks. So he'd sent a cleaning crew to the ranch yesterday, something he'd insisted on when he'd last talked to Sandra. He knew she'd be uneasy about having her guests see dusty furniture or find her kitchen anything other than spotless. She'd reluctantly agreed and thanked him, saying only that her time was limited these days.

So were her finances, which was why he insisted upon paying for everything. Dana had picked up the tab for the party decorations and the cake, but he planned to reimburse those expenses as soon as he saw her, which would be in a few short minutes.

He and Rosie had almost reached the Leaning L. He'd planned to arrive before the first guest did, but an unexpected business call from a client in New York had thrown him off schedule.

"Is Dana going to be there?" Rosie asked from the backseat.

The child had referred to Dana as Mommy nearly

every day for the past two weeks. Why had that changed?

Had she sensed the issue that had cropped up between them on Wednesday night? He hadn't thought she could be so perceptive, but then again, Rosie continued to surprise him. Either way, he was determined to square things with Dana today and they'd be lovers before dawn. Even the *C* word, *commitment*, didn't sound so bad when it came to her.

"I'm sure Dana is already there. She's making the birthday cake, remember?" Kieran glanced in the rearview mirror and watched Rosie nod in agreement.

He would let Dana know that he'd changed that *1* to a *2* on his RSVP card. He'd have to endure some major taunts at the wedding and long after it was over, but she was worth it.

Moments later, he and Rosie turned into the driveway. He didn't see Dana's car, though. That was odd. She knew how important this party was to Rosie.

He shook off his momentary concern. She'd probably had to stop by a store to pick up something at the last minute.

After parking near the barn, he got out of the car and unbuckled Rosie. "How does it feel to be four years old?"

She beamed and took his hand.

Kelly and several of her teenage friends greeted them before they could walk ten paces toward the house.

"There's Princess Rosie," Kelly said. "Come with us. We're going to get you ready to meet your guests.

We have crowns and tiaras to pass out to everyone when they arrive."

Kieran thought about following them into the house, but since he expected Dana at any moment, he waited in the yard. That would give him the perfect opportunity to apologize in private.

Five minutes later, when the first guests arrived in a minivan, Dana still hadn't shown up. He welcomed the mother and her little girl then pointed them to the porch, where Rosie and the teenagers were waiting to hand out the tiaras and crowns.

By the time a third carload of party guests arrived, he decided he'd better call Dana to check on her. But before he could take out his cell phone, he spotted Elaine and Michael Wagner getting out of a white sedan that had seen better days.

He greeted them with a smile. "I'm glad you could make it."

Elaine, who was helping Michael from his car seat, said, "We wouldn't have missed it for the world. This party is all Mikey's been talking about for days."

By the time she pulled out a gift bag and shut the passenger door, Kieran began to realize Dana might be a no-show.

How could she disappoint Rosie like that? She might be angry at him—and he deserved it. But why take it out on a child?

He headed to the house himself, guilt warring with anger, and entered the kitchen, where Sandra was preparing a pot of coffee.

"Have you heard anything from Dana?" he asked.

"Yes, she woke up with a terrible headache. But what a trooper. She drove out early this morning to bring the cake and cupcakes as well as a gift bag for Rosie."

So she hadn't ditched the party. A headache was a reasonable excuse. Or had she only feigned illness?

He had no idea what to think, let alone do. He wanted to talk to her, but he couldn't very well leave when the party was just getting started.

Before he could quiz Sandra and ask how Dana looked, whether she might need something—or someone—to check in on her, Elaine entered the kitchen. "Sandra, is there anything I can do to help? Dana didn't want you to lift a finger."

So Dana had asked someone to cover for her, following through on her promise to help since she couldn't be here herself. Her kindness and consideration was both amazing and touching.

"Go on out to the living room and enjoy the guests," Kieran told Sandra. "Elaine and I can handle things."

"What would I do without you?" Sandra asked.

Kieran tossed her a grin. "I could ask you the same thing. You've given me some of the best meals I've ever had. And I consider you and Sam part of my family now."

She nodded, unshed tears glistening in her eyes, and walked away, leaving Kieran and Elaine alone.

"Thanks for offering to help us out," Kieran told her.

"I don't mind at all," she said. "In fact, I was flattered when Dana called me on Thursday and asked me to step in for her."

Kieran froze in his tracks. So Dana had known two days ago that she wasn't going to attend the party?

Damn, he'd been more of an ass than he'd thought.

"Is something wrong?" Elaine asked, as she prepared a tray with cream, sugar, a carafe and disposable foam cups.

He shook off his surprise. "No, I was just having a..."

"Senior moment?" Elaine asked. "I know all about those."

Actually, he was going to say that he was having an epiphany.

"Before I married Michael's father," she said, "I lived with my great-grandparents. My grandpa had dementia and his health was failing, so I took care of him at the end."

"That must have been hard on you."

"It was. I hated to see him struggle to remember, but I was glad that I could be with him during his last days. In fact, since I need to find work so I can move out of my parents' house and find a place of our own, I might apply for a job at a local hospice. I don't have a college education or any real experience—other than being a mom and a caretaker."

A thought came to mind, a solution that might work out for all of them. "Have you ever considered being a nanny?"

"No, not really. My parents' home is pretty small, so I can't really watch kids there. And if I went to work at the family's house, I'd have to take Michael with me. Most parents wouldn't want to have an extra child at their place when they're at work."

Actually, Kieran wouldn't mind that. And if Elaine not only looked after Rosie at the ranch while he was at the office, she could also be a caretaker for the Lawsons. They needed someone to look after them, too. They also had a small guesthouse, where Zach had once lived.

This might be the perfect solution for everyone involved.

"Let's have a chat after the party," he said. "I've got a thought simmering that might solve your problem."

He just hoped he'd get another brilliant idea. One that would help him solve the huge predicament he'd created with Dana.

Chapter Twelve

The party was finally over, and the last guest had gone home. Elaine had volunteered to help Kieran clean up, and he'd taken her up on the offer. She'd also agreed to watch Rosie for him later, so she'd followed him to his place.

After he let her and the kids inside, she said, "Take all the time you need. We'll be fine." Elaine gave him a grin. "I can even stay overnight if you need me."

Kieran thanked her, then drove straight to Dana's house. He hadn't called ahead, so he hoped she was home. He'd thought briefly about picking up a bouquet of roses as a peace offering, like he'd done the last time he'd apologized to her, but now that he'd finally realized how he felt about her, he just wanted to get there as fast as possible and tell her.

He rang the bell, shifting his weight from foot to foot as he waited what seemed like forever for her to answer the door. Finally, she stood before him, her hair glossy and flowing over her shoulders and down her back. But the moment she laid eyes on him, she crossed her arms as if to stand her ground.

He wasted no time with small talk.

"I'm sorry," he said. "I was a jerk the other night, and you didn't deserve it. I hurt you when you found out I hadn't planned to take you to Sophie's wedding. That wasn't my intention."

"Forget about it. That's not what upset me. Not really."

Either way, he'd screwed up. "You have every right to be angry with me, and I want to make things right."

"Don't worry about it. I don't want to attend that wedding with you, anyway."

Fixing this wasn't going to be as easy as he'd hoped it would be, and he doubted that flowers would have helped. She was clearly angry. "I didn't come here to invite you to be my date to my sister's wedding."

Her lips parted, and disbelief stretched across her face. "I see. So it's over between us?"

"I hope not."

He offered her a smile, but worry marred her brow, suggesting that she wasn't ready for their relationship to end, either.

Kieran chuckled. "I should have worded that better. In fact, let me start over. My feelings for you were unsettling and hard for me to admit. I didn't want it to happen and I fought it every step of the way."

"I'm not surprised. Your dating habits aren't a big secret."

"It was more than that. I felt as though I was stepping into the life Zach had set up for himself, the life he deserved. And I was wracked by guilt. Then, after a while, I was able to envision my own future—if you were a part of it."

"I told you that Zach and I weren't that close. We never even slept together. It was his family that drew me in. I lost my parents when I was young, and Sandra came close to filling a maternal role for me. That's why I continued to see Zach, even when I knew marriage wasn't in our future. He knew it, too, but he appreciated my help with Rosie—just like you seem to."

"This isn't about Rosie," Kieran said. "It's about *me*. And it's about the feeling that's grown so strong it's going to burst out of me if I don't tell you about it."

She seemed to sway back, as if his words had struck a sensitive chord, but she quickly recovered. "That's hard to believe."

He could see why she might feel that way. "When you walked out the other night, I let you go because I thought it would be best for everyone involved. Rosie was calling you Mommy. And I was having visions of you day and night—and not just in bed, but your smile, your gentle touch. Your laugh." He raked a hand through his hair. "I'd spent so long being a carefree bachelor that I didn't think I could handle a real, committed relationship. And the fact that you had me reconsidering that scared the hell out of me."

She unfolded her arms. "So that's why you didn't stop me from leaving and why you didn't call afterward?"

He nodded. "It took a while for me to wrap my head around the fact that I don't want to be alone any longer. You've brought something into my life that I've never had before—a real sense of love and family."

"Oh, come on, Kieran. Other than my friend Monica, you have one of the biggest families I know."

"Maybe so. But in spite of the number of siblings I have, I've never been all that happy. And I doubt I ever will be. Not without you in my life."

Dana couldn't believe her eyes when Kieran showed up at her door. And now she couldn't believe her ears.

"It may seem a bit sudden," he said, "but I know what's in my heart. I've never felt anything like this, but I know what's going on. I fell in love with you, Dana. And all I want is for the two of us—I mean, the *three* of us—to be together. Not just tonight, but for the rest of our lives."

Dana continued to stand in the doorway, too stunned by his words to move, to even react. To say his revelation had completely blindsided her would be a gross understatement. She had to remind herself to breathe. He *loved* her? That in itself was hard to wrap her mind around, but for the *rest* of their lives? That sounded as if...

"Aren't you going to invite me into the house?" he asked.

His question pulled her out of her reverie and she stepped aside and held open the door for him to enter.

"I hope you'll forgive me for being a little slow on the uptake," he said as he walked into the living room. "It took time for me to figure things out—and to propose a solution."

"I'm listening."

"I know you're not the type for a sexual fling, which is the only kind of relationship I used to have. But not anymore. I only want one woman in my life from now on, and that's you."

This conversation was becoming surreal. Maybe it was time to give herself a pinch.

"Are you sure?" she asked.

He smiled at her. "Absolutely. That's why I didn't want you to be my date at that wedding. I want you to be my bride."

"I don't understand," she said.

"Let's get married on the same day, in the same place and at the same time, as Sophie and Mason."

Actually, she liked the sound of that. But he couldn't be serious. Still, she'd never seen his face so lit up.

When she didn't respond either way, he dropped to one knee, reached into his pocket and pulled out a small velvet box. He flicked open the lid, revealing a sparkling diamond that had to be two carats, if not more.

She gasped, then lifted her hand to her throat and

gazed at him in disbelief. She'd never seen anything like it. For a poor girl who'd grown up without a family of her own, you'd think she'd just been given the Hope Diamond.

"I don't know what to say."

"A *yes* would make me the happiest man in the world. In fact, I'd marry you today, if you'd have me."

He was serious.

And she was…thrilled.

"Then yes," she said. "I'll marry you."

Kieran pulled the ring from the box, dazzling her with the romantic gesture and the sparkle, and she lifted her left hand to let him slide it on her finger.

What a turn of events. Even in her wildest dreams, when she'd lain in bed at night, envisioning Kieran professing his love, she'd never expected it to be like this—so romantic, so sweet. And accompanied by a proposal.

"I love you, too," she said. "And I don't want to wait, either. But I can't see how we can pull off a double wedding."

She'd need to find a dress—and something fancy, especially if they got married at the Driskill Hotel, with his friends and family in attendance.

"Besides," she added, "Sophie and Mason's invitations have already gone out. And they were so perfect, so formal… We'd just be an add-on."

"I already ran this by Sophie, and she thinks we'll make an amazing addition to the ceremony. And as for the invitations, we'll create our own and email them to our guests."

"But…there's another problem," she said, considering the wording Sophie and Mason had used. "I don't have parents to list at the top of our invitation."

Kieran seemed to think about that, but only for a moment. "I have a much better idea."

She tilted her head. "What's that?"

"Picture this." He lifted his hands, his thumb and index fingers creating a box shape. "Miss Rosabelle Lawson requests the honor of your presence at the wedding of her new Mommy and Daddy—Miss Dana Trevino and Mr. Kieran Fortune Robinson."

Tears filled Dana's eyes. "That's perfect. I love it!"

"You're perfect. And I love you." He reached out for her and pulled her into his arms.

Then he said, "All you need to do is tell me where you want to go on our honeymoon."

She stiffened, drawing back so she could catch his gaze. "Getting married with Sophie and Mason at the Driskill Hotel would be a dream come true for me, but we can't go anywhere for very long, especially if we have to leave town."

"Why not?"

"What about Rosie? She wouldn't be happy staying with just anyone for longer than a night. And then there's Sam and Sandra to consider. You and I are all the family they have left. What if something should happen while we're gone? What if they need us?"

"I've got that covered."

She couldn't see how. The guy might be rich, but you couldn't buy affection and peace of mind.

"I hired the perfect nanny," he said. "And she's going to start work tomorrow."

"But you don't work on Sunday."

"I won't need her to watch Rosie at my house. She's going to live at the ranch."

She wasn't following, and her brows knitted in confusion.

Kieran smiled. "I hired a caregiver to look after Sam and Sandra. And she'll also be my nanny. Whenever I need a sitter, I'll take Rosie there. It's the perfect solution. And Sandra and Sam are delighted with the setup."

"Who is this woman? And when did you hire her?"

"It's Elaine Wagner, Mikey's mother. And I hired her today."

"And she agreed to look after Sam and Sandra, too?"

"She was thrilled when I suggested it. And so was Sandra, especially since she'll be seeing more of Rosie."

Dana couldn't stifle the grin that stole across her face. "You are a true problem solver, Mr. Fortune."

He laughed. "Well, there is one little problem…"

"Uh-oh. What's that?"

"I promised Rosie that I would drive over to that empty lot by the school and look for a big, brown, dirty dog named Teddy."

"Seriously? What are you going to do if you find that stray?"

"Take it to the ranch. But don't think badly of me if I admit that I'm hopeful he's already found another home."

She stepped back into the circle of his arms. "Kieran, you are truly amazing. I'm going to love being married to you."

Then she kissed him, thoroughly and deeply. When they finally came up for air, she led him to her bedroom. It was time to celebrate the love they'd just professed.

Dana had never been happier. After spending the night with her new fiancé and making love several times, each one more amazing than the last, she'd kissed Kieran goodbye. Then he went to his place to relieve Elaine and pick up Rosie.

Over an early morning cup of coffee, they'd decided Kieran and Rosie would move in with Dana until they found a new house, something bigger and with a roomy yard. Kieran would be giving up his downtown condo.

In the meantime, she spent the morning cleaning out the guest room, especially the closet, to make room for Rosie's clothes and toys. Her heart soared at the thought of having her new family together under the same roof.

Kieran had called a couple hours ago to let her know that he and Rosie had a few errands to run. That was just as well. Dana wanted to have the room ready when they arrived.

She'd no more than carried the last box out to the garage when her cell phone rang. She thought it might be Kieran, calling her with an update, but it was his sister Sophie instead.

"I just heard the good news," Sophie said. "Kieran told me you agreed to the double wedding, and I wanted to let you know how happy Mason and I are that you'll be sharing our special day."

It was mind-boggling. In less than twenty-four hours, Dana had acquired a fiancé who would soon be her husband, and a daughter. Now she had a sister, the first of many siblings.

Dana smiled. "Kieran and I are looking forward to it."

"If you're free tonight," Sophie said, "I thought we could all get together. Rosie, too, of course. That way, we can talk more about it."

"That works for me. I'll check with Kieran to make sure he doesn't have anything else going on."

"Let me know for sure, but I'll plan for us to have dinner at my place around six."

After ending the call, Dana considered all that needed to be done to prepare for a dream wedding. How would she ever be ready in just over a week?

She pulled a notepad from her desk drawer, as well as a pencil, so she could jot down each upcoming chore and give it a completion date.

The first thing on her to-do list was to call Monica and tell her the good news.

"Oh my gosh," Monica said when Dana got her

on the phone. "You're going to marry one of the *Fortunes*?"

"Actually," Dana said, as she plopped down in her easy chair for a conversation that was sure to go into overtime, "I'm marrying the most handsome, generous and incredible man in the world. He just happens to carry the Fortune name. But believe me, I wouldn't care if he was a Smith or a Jones."

"That's awesome, Dana. I'm so happy for you."

"Good, because I need a favor. I want you to be my maid of honor. Hopefully, you can get the time off from the library so you can help me pull things together."

"One of my assistants is out on maternity leave, so I'm not sure how long I can be gone. But I wouldn't miss your wedding for the world. Besides, I want to help you find something old, something new, something borrowed and something blue."

Dana held the phone with her right hand and rested the left on the armrest, the diamond engagement ring sparkling. She really was going to have to pinch herself for a reality check.

"You know me," Dana said. "I'm big on traditions, so I'll definitely be using that one. It's just too bad that I don't have my mother's wedding gown to wear. That would've given me the perfect 'something old.' But I'll just have to look for a lace handkerchief at an upcoming estate sale."

"Wait," Monica said. "I've got a better idea. My mom wore my *abuelita*'s wedding dress when she got married, and she's been saving it for me. Why don't you wear that?"

"But that's your family tradition."

"Come on, Dana. You're like a sister to me. I'd love to see you walk down the aisle in something that means so much to our family. I'd have to alter it anyway, and you're about my mom's size."

Tears welled in Dana's eyes, then spilled onto her cheeks. "I'd be so honored to wear that dress. I promise to take special care of it."

"I know you will. And now you've got something old *and* borrowed."

"That's true. Maybe I can go to a bridal shop and find a blue garter. That would take care of new and blue."

Monica laughed. "Better yet, how about some sexy blue panties?"

Now it was Dana's turn to laugh. "We'll have to go shopping together and see what we can find." She again looked at her ring, which stood out prominently on her finger. Okay, so it wasn't anywhere near as big as the Hope Diamond. But it reflected a heart *filled* with hope. Not to mention love and everything that was right in the world.

"What about your honeymoon?" Monica asked. "Where are you guys going?"

"At first, I assumed we'd just spend time alone at home. But thanks to Rosie's awesome new nanny, we're going to be able to leave her in good hands. So this morning, over breakfast, we decided on Paris. Can you believe I finally get to visit that city? It's filled with so much history and culture. I'd stay a month, if I could. But since Kieran and I both have work, we're only going for ten days."

"I'm so happy for you. Kieran sounds like a real keeper. I can't wait to meet him. Hey, does he have a single brother or friend who's attracted to petite brunettes?"

"I'll definitely scope out any suitable prospects. I'd love to see you more often."

Monica laughed. "After my last relationship, which turned out to be a dud, I'm holding out for a hero like the ones I've read about in romance novels."

"Maybe a handsome swashbuckler?" Dana asked.

"Or better yet, how about a Scottish laird?"

Down the street, the sound of a familiar diesel engine grew louder. "Listen, Monica. I'll have to call you later. Kieran and Rosie are back from the groomer."

"The *groomer*?" Monica asked. "What'd you do, inherit a pet with your new family?"

"Um, sort of. I haven't met him yet, but from what Kieran told me after finding him in an empty lot this morning, he's a big, goofy dog who looks like he's half wolfhound and part who-knows-what."

"You're adopting a stray that you don't know anything about?" Monica asked.

"Kieran said he's pretty friendly. And just for the record, he'll live on the Leaning L. That's where we'll be taking him—after I meet him, of course."

After promising Monica that they'd talk more later, Dana disconnected the line and went to greet her family.

* * *

Kieran had never been a dog person, but a promise was a promise. After picking up Rosie, who'd had the time of her life spending the night with Elaine and Mikey, he'd driven to her school to look for Teddy. And sure enough, they found him.

The big mutt ran right up to Rosie as if she was his long lost littermate. As she hugged him tightly, in spite of his dirty fur, he placed a big sloppy kiss on her face.

It was going to be difficult to say no to this child, which was why he'd placed several calls until he found a groomer that was open on Sundays. After dropping off Teddy for a much-needed bath and clipping, they'd gone to Pet Depot and purchased a collar, leash, food and a bed.

Teddy looked like a brand-new dog when they picked him up, and now he rode in the back of Kieran's Mercedes to Dana's house, panting and thumping his tail against the seat.

After pulling into Dana's driveway and shutting off the ignition, Kieran scanned the well-kept yard and cozy house. For the first time in his life, he felt as though he'd finally come home.

"Can I hold Teddy's leash?" Rosie asked.

The dog had been so rambunctious after being caged at the groomers that he would probably knock her off her feet.

"I'll tell you what," Kieran said. "Let's ask Dana if she wants to take a walk with us. Then, after Teddy gets some of his energy out, you can hold on to him."

"Okay. But don't call her Dana. Her name is going to be Mommy now, remember?"

"You got it, sweetie."

After they all got out of the car, including Teddy who'd nearly jerked Kieran's arm out of the socket as he leaped to the ground, they headed to the front door.

"Mommy" met them with a warm smile before they reached the porch, and Rosie introduced her to Teddy.

"Hey," Kieran said to Dana. "I know you're riding with us to take Teddy to the ranch, but he's going to need to take a little walk first. Would you like to join us for a trek around the neighborhood?"

"I can't think of anything I'd rather do than spend a Sunday afternoon with my family."

Damn. He loved that woman.

"Then let's go," he said.

Dana reached for her key, which she left on a little hook near the door, and locked up the house. Then they headed down the quiet, tree-lined street, birds chirping, the sun shining.

He wasn't sure how long they'd live at her house. That was up to Dana. But it didn't matter. Home would always be wherever she was.

As they turned the corner and headed down another street, Kieran wondered who was happier— Teddy, Rosie, Dana or him. All he knew was that he had enough money to buy anything he'd ever wanted, yet nothing he'd ever wanted had fulfilled him like the woman who'd just slipped her hand into his.

"It's going to be a beautiful day," Dana said.

"It's going to be a beautiful *life*," he corrected.

She squeezed his hand and tossed him a loving smile.

"Can I hold on to Teddy now?" Rosie asked.

The dog had settled into a gentle walk, so Kieran passed the red leash to her, and they continued on their way.

The sun was warm and bright, and a cool spring breeze rustled in the treetops.

"Look," Dana said softly. She pointed to Rosie's shoulder, where a monarch butterfly had landed, its orange-and-black wings fluttering.

He was reminded of the butterfly at the funeral. It was almost as if Zach was letting him know that he'd cast his blessing on this new family.

At least, it seemed that way. And even though it might sound weird, Kieran chose to believe that's exactly what was happening.

He pondered the fragile little butterfly that had once been a caterpillar. Just like its metamorphosis, something inside Kieran had changed, too. At one time, he'd feared fatherhood and marriage. But now, thanks to Dana, he couldn't wait for their upcoming wedding, the tuxedoes and white lace, the promises they'd make—and the little flower girl who'd be a huge part of it all. And for their happy-ever-after to start.

For a guy who'd once been a dedicated bachelor, Kieran had turned over a new leaf. He couldn't imagine his life without Dana and Rosie. In fact, he looked forward to the holidays, something he'd dreaded in the past, and to showering them with gifts of love.

Maybe there'd also be a new baby or two in the future.

He liked that idea. Liked it a lot. Because he couldn't imagine love or family getting much better than this.

* * * * *

Don't miss the next installment of the
Harlequin Special Edition continuity
THE FORTUNES OF TEXAS:
THE SECRET FORTUNES

When Olivia Fortune Robinson and
Alejandro Mendoza are forced to fake an
engagement, will they be able to tell the difference
between fantasy and reality when their pretend
arrangement becomes an affair of the heart?

Look for
FORTUNE'S SURPRISE ENGAGEMENT
by Nancy Robards Thompson

On sale May 2017, wherever Harlequin books
and ebooks are sold.

Dear Reader,

This month—April 2017—marks the 35th anniversary for Harlequin Special Edition! Perhaps it's as hard for you, the reader, to believe this as it is for us, the team that has been presenting this warm, wonderful and relatable series of books for all these years. And while some of us are newer than others, the one thing that has always been consistent is that the Harlequin Special Edition lineup has always reached out and grabbed you, made you want to read more, made you look forward to what comes next.

April 2017 is a great illustration of this. We have *New York Times* bestselling author Brenda Novak in Harlequin Special Edition for the first time with *Finding Our Forever*, alongside our almost-brand-new author Katie Meyer with another in her Proposals in Paradise series, *The Groom's Little Girls*. We have *USA TODAY* bestselling and beloved authors Marie Ferrarella (*Meant to be Married*) and Judy Duarte in our next Fortunes of Texas: The Secret Fortunes story (*From Fortune to Family Man*). And if it's glamour, glitz and sparkle you want with your romance, look no further than *The Princess Problem* (next in the Drake Diamonds trilogy) by Teri Wilson.

We have moved through the last thirty-five years giving you, the reader, stories that warmed your heart and curled your toes, and we are just getting started! So happy anniversary...and here's to the next thirty-five!

Happy Reading,

Gail Chasan
Senior Editor, Harlequin Special Edition

Available April 18, 2017

#2545 THE LAWMAN'S CONVENIENT BRIDE
The Bravos of Justice Creek • by Christine Rimmer
Jody Bravo has vowed to raise her baby alone and do it right. But Sheriff
Seth Yancy, whose deceased stepbrother is the father of Jody's child, is going
to protect and look after the baby and Jody—whether she wants his help or not.

#2546 CHARM SCHOOL FOR COWBOYS
Hurley's Homestyle Kitchen • by Meg Maxwell
When pregnant Emma Hurley starts a charm school for rancher Jake Morrow's
lovelorn cowboys, she never expected to enter into a fake engagement with
Jake. But when her father threatens to sell her family farm, Emma will do
whatever it takes to save it, even risk her heart!

#2547 HER KIND OF DOCTOR
Men of the West • by Stella Bagwell
Nurse Paige Winters and Dr. Luke Sherman have butted heads since they
started working in the ER together. But after she finally gives him a piece of
her mind and switches floors, Luke realizes Paige is much more than just
another nurse, and he's determined to prove he's exactly her kind of doctor!

#2548 FORTUNE'S SURPRISE ENGAGEMENT
The Fortunes of Texas: The Secret Fortunes
by Nancy Robards Thompson
Olivia Fortune Robinson has to prove to her sister that love is real, stat! So she
convinces everyone that she and Alejandro Mendoza are madly in love. And
when he proposes, she's just as shocked as everyone else. But his past loss
and her present cynicism threaten to keep this surprise engagement from
becoming the real thing.

#2549 THE LAST SINGLE GARRETT
Those Engaging Garretts! • by Brenda Harlen
When Josh Slater finds himself entrusted with the care of his three nieces
for the summer, he's forced to rely on his best friend's younger sister,
Tristyn Garrett, for help. But their attraction has simmered below the surface
for twelve years, and a summer spent on an RV road trip looks to be their
breaking point...

#2550 THE BRONC RIDER'S BABY
Rocking Chair Rodeo • by Judy Duarte
Former rodeo cowboy Nate Gallagher has just discovered he's the daddy of
a newborn baby girl—and starts falling for Anna Reynolds, the pretty social
worker assigned to assess whether he's true father material! Nate knows the
stakes are higher than ever. He's not just risking his heart, but a future for his
daughter.

SPECIAL EXCERPT FROM

HARLEQUIN®

SPECIAL EDITION

When Sheriff Seth Yancy finds out Jody Bravo is
pregnant with his late brother's child, he's determined
to stay in their life, even if that means making her a very
convenient bride...

Read on for a sneak preview of
THE LAWMAN'S CONVENIENT BRIDE,
the next book in New York Times
bestselling author Christine Rimmer's,
THE BRAVOS OF JUSTICE CREEK miniseries.

"Mirabelle's?" It was a new restaurant in town, a small, cozy
place with white tablecloths and crystal chandeliers and a chef
from New York. Everyone said the food was really good and
the service impeccable.

"I heard it was good," he said. "Would you rather go
somewhere else?"

"I just didn't know we were doing that."

"Doing what?"

"Going through with the date."

He set down his fork. "We're doing it." His voice was deep
and rough, and his velvet-brown gaze caught hers and held it.

It just wasn't fair that the guy was so damn hot. *Not
happening*, she reminded herself. *Don't get ideas.* "What about
Marybeth?"

"It's only a few hours. Get a sitter. Maybe one of your sisters
or maybe your mom?"

"Ma? Please."

"She did raise five children, didn't she?"

"She's probably off on her next cruise already."

"A babysitter, Jody. I'm sure you can find one."

"But Marybeth is barely four weeks old."

"Jody. We're going. Stop making excuses."

She sagged back in her chair. "Why are you so determined about this?"

"Because I want to take you out."

"But…you don't go out, remember? There's no point because it can't go anywhere. Not to mention, I live in Broomtail County, and what if it got messy with me?"

"Too late." He was almost smiling. She could see that increasingly familiar twitch at the corner of his mouth. "It's already messy with you."

"I am not joking, Seth."

"Neither am I. I want to be with you, Jody. And not just as a friend."

"B-but I…" God. She was sputtering. And why did she suddenly feel light as a breath of air, as if she was floating on moonbeams? "You want to be with me? But you don't do that. You've made that very clear."

"You're right. I didn't do that. Until now. But things have changed."

"Because of Marybeth, you mean?"

"Yeah, because of Marybeth. And because of you, too. Because of the way you are. Strong and honest and smart and so pretty. Because we've got something going on, you and me. Something good. I'm through pretending that we're friends and nothing more. Are you telling me I'm the only one who feels that way?"

"I just…" Her pulse raced and her cheeks felt too hot. She'd promised herself that nothing like this would happen, that she wouldn't get her hopes up.

She needed to be careful. She could end up with her heart in pieces all over again.

Don't miss
THE LAWMAN'S CONVENIENT BRIDE
by Christine Rimmer, available May 2017 wherever
Harlequin® Special Edition books and ebooks are sold.

www.Harlequin.com

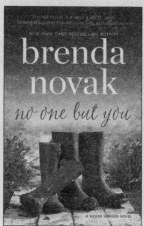